BOOKS

SOLDIERS OF ARTEMIS

ARTEMIS BOOK 3

ROBERT C. JAMES

PROLOGUE

"Can you hear me?"

Vernon stared across the enormous infirmary, past the other wounded pilots and through a transparent screen into the surgical ward. He could hear Lieutenant Argyle speaking, but nothing of what he was saying registered. Little had since their confrontation with Bolaran forces earlier in the day, when he and the rest of the Twelfth Fleet had their pants pulled down by the enemy. As Lieutenant Corina Harvey lay unconscious in the surgical ward, hooked up to every medical contraption imaginable, what took place hours earlier didn't seem to matter. None of it.

"Hey, Captain?"

Vernon snapped out of his daze, and his eyes slowly drifted from Corina to Lieutenant Argyle in the bed next to him. The fifth member of his fighter squadron was injured, like the rest of them. Luckily, he'd escaped the battle with no more than a fractured leg. The doctor said he'd be back on his feet within a couple of days, while Vernon, who'd dislocated his shoulder and smashed his knee open, was told he'd be out of action for at least a week.

He hoped Fighter Corps Command would give him and his pilots the time to heal, but with the war between the Bolarans escalating, he worried they'd be thrown to the wolves as soon as they were able. He didn't fear going out there. At the end of the day, being inside the cockpit was what he was born to do. But that wasn't necessarily the case for the rest of the pilots under his command.

"Are you there or not?" Argyle asked him again.

Vernon scowled. "I'm here."

The young lieutenant shifted in his bed, attempting to get comfortable. "You're worried about her, aren't you?"

Vernon peered back across at Corina. "What the hell do you think?"

"There's nothing you could've done. There were a lot more of them than we expected."

"That doesn't make me feel any better. You're all my pilots. It's my job to protect you."

"You have eleven pilots under your command. You can't look after all of us. Besides, Corina can take after herself. She just got unlucky." Argyle clicked his fingers, trying to recapture Vernon's attention. "She'll pull through. We've got the best doctors in the Empire here."

Vernon hoped he was right. As he turned his head, he peered out amongst the stars beyond the viewport of one of the Empire's most storied carriers. The crew aboard her and those throughout the rest of the fleet were still licking their wounds. Many had lost their lives today, and in the coming weeks no doubt more would join them.

"Besides," Argyle continued. "Haven't you heard? The emperor's here."

"What the hell are you talking about?" Vernon scoffed.

"When that hot nurse let me go for a walk on my crutches earlier, I overheard someone say the emperor's fleet have rendezvoused with us. Word has it, he's here to meet the troops."

"That's preposterous."

Argyle shrugged. "That's what I heard."

"You're much too gullible sometimes. Once we're out of this, I'll have to give you a lesson on how the real world works."

The lieutenant was about to protest. Instead, the door at the far end of the recovery ward swooshed open, and the quiet confines containing the near one hundred wounded pilots became a ruckus with armed soldiers entering the confines. A trio of the carrier's senior officers followed, along with another squad of guards.

Argyle leaned over as much as he could. "What did I tell you?"

Vernon didn't answer his cocky young pilot, instead holding his gaze on the circus walking through the door behind the initial visitors. There were at least twenty in the entourage, ranging from lowly sergeants, to some generals who'd tagged along for the ride. In the heart of them were but two civilian figures. One much more recognizable than the other.

Vernon had never met the emperor in person before. All he'd heard were stories. But there was indeed an aura about him, as all the rumors had claimed. Strangely, he was shorter than everyone around him. But it didn't matter. There was a harshness in his eyes that demanded complete and utter attention.

The emperor, with the other civilian, went from bed to bed while his guards took station at all the exits, keeping a close eye on the proceedings. What dismay had been in the many pilots' faces transformed to joy with a brief word with the highest office in the Empire. Eventually the group reached Vernon, and the emperor stepped to his side. The taller civilian stood at the foot of the bed and examined the name on the monitor. He moved to the emperor and whispered something in his ear.

The emperor's eyes lit up, and he smiled at Vernon warmly. "Councilor McCrae here tells me you're Captain Charles Vernon."

"Uh, yes, sir," Vernon stammered.

"The Captain Charles Vernon who recorded victories at Santar, Voreki Prime, and Milner II?"

Vernon nodded, recalling the grueling campaigns that had taken place in the outer regions with Arcadian forces pressing toward the Bolaran core worlds. They were the same memories that visited him every night in all his nightmares.

"It's an honor to meet you, Captain." The emperor noticed Vernon's bandaged knee. "I've been watching your career closely. You've been awarded many medals and led many successful missions for the Empire. I don't think it's out of line to say you've become the Empire's greatest pilot."

Vernon didn't know how to take the praise. He regarded the expectant faces surrounding him, from the councilor and the generals, to the carrier's officers. Praise was something he was never comfortable with, but he had to be mindful of the company he was keeping. "Thank you, sir. I just wish we'd been able to do more. A lot of good people died today."

The emperor nodded. "While many good soldiers of the Empire may have given their lives here, take solace in the fact they didn't die in vain."

Vernon furrowed his brow, and he glanced past the

emperor at Corina. She remained deathly still in the surgical ward. "Sir?"

"Your attack on Hectar IV was but a small part of a campaign that's been months in its preparations." The emperor sat on his bed, being careful not to crush Vernon's injured knee. "While the Twelfth Fleet were engaging the enemy at Hectar, the Third and Seventh fleets tore through the front lines at Kiljara. As we speak, reinforcements have joined them, and they're now making a run toward the Bolaran core worlds."

"We were a decoy?" Vernon's gaze remained glued to Corina. For a moment, everything around him seemed to disappear, apart from the throaty voice of his leader.

"You did well today, Captain." The emperor put his hand on Vernon's. There was a coldness about it, as if ice filled his veins. "The Empire thanks you."

With that, the short-statured man and his entourage moved on to Lieutenant Argyle and beyond, giving the rest of the pilots the boost in morale they so desperately needed. Vernon clenched his fists and gnashed his teeth.

"Well, that was something, wasn't it?" Argyle leaned back on his pillow. "My folks will never believe me when I tell them I got to meet the emperor."

Vernon was about to tell him to shut up, but some activity in the surgical bay caught his eye. Corina began to convulse, and all the cables they'd hooked up to her flailed around her. Doctors and nurses appeared out of nowhere and got to work on her in a frenzy.

"Corina..." He sat up and threw his sheet aside.

Argyle said nothing, obviously noticing what was happening, too. Vernon stumbled under the stress of his healing knee with a sharp pain pulsating from it and running up the length of his body.

He winced all the way to the screen of the surgical

ward and fell onto it, placing his hand on the glass. Trays of medical equipment were wheeled to Corina's side, and surgical instruments were exchanged between the doctors and nurses at breakneck speed. It all became a blur, and the surrounding noise from the excitement of the emperor's visit merged into a piercing whine.

Like it was when she was fit and healthy, Corina fought like hell against the odds. He could only imagine what she'd gone through when she'd ejected from her cockpit after a trio of Bolaran fighters stalked her down and destroyed her craft.

Whatever drugs the surgeons had given her to calm her down did little to stop her struggle. Her eyes fluttered, and her arms flailed.

Then everything stopped.

Her body gave out, and her head collapsed into her pillow. The doctors with blood up to their armpits stared at each other and checked the readings on the medical monitors.

Their gloves came off.

The red-stained latex launched across the surgical bay into the trash, and the nurses pulled a sheet over Corina's body.

Vernon fell to the floor.

He glared at the emperor and those who had come with him to lick his boots. But he was gone, along with the rest of them.

Back to his palace on Arcadia.

Away from the war.

Away from the death.

ONE

Yevgeny Novikov was never one to shy away from hard work. He'd been born on the farms, raised on the farms, and worked on the farms since the day he could stand. He'd toiled on his parents' property for as many years as he'd had birthdays, until the day it became his own. The man had seen and done it all. Every weather event imaginable had been thrown at him, from the coldest of winters where the insidious black ice destroyed an entire season of crops, to the most destructive of summers where it got so hot the corn popped in the afternoon sun.

He crouched in the middle of the field, brushing away the sweat from his forehead, his weary knees nearly buckling under him. A bout of light-headedness struck, and a cramp throbbed in his right thigh. He reached for his pocket for some salt tablets, but they were empty. He wondered if he'd used them all up or if he'd just forgotten to bring them with him. Yevgeny sighed and rubbed his hand over the soil. It was as dry as he'd ever seen it.

The drought had been a long one. Usually, Gelbrana could get through the wild swings in climate due to the phenomenal planet-wide water vapor system which searched out any wetness below the surface so the farms scattered across the colony had a half a fighting chance. But with the onset of the war, any water that was extracted was shared throughout the Outer Rim to those who needed it. There were some days Yevgeny resented the policy, but he had to remind himself it would be a hell of a lot worse if the Empire took complete control.

Yevgeny finally stood, wincing from the lingering cramp, and trudged to his speeder. He turned the key and checked the battery. There was little charge in the vehicle, but luckily just enough to get him back home. He set off and rounded the crops on the far edge of his property and made his way to the heart of the vast mass of Novikov Ranch. From behind the controls, he could see the entire breadth of his land. It should have been something to enjoy, but he remembered as a child riding in the back of the old clunker and feeling almost claustrophobic because of how tall the crops were around him. There hadn't been seasons that profitable in a very long time.

He reached the rickety old ranch house and parked the speeder out the front of the place he called home. The two-story abode was looking worse for wear these days, with the heat peeling at the paint and sun beginning to buckle some of the outer structure. It was still livable. Unfortunately, in a few summers it probably wouldn't be.

Yevgeny jumped from the speeder and traipsed up the steps and through the door into the much cooler confines of his house. His air-conditioning system might have been twenty years old, but it still got the job done. Anything had to be better than the typical Gelbrana climate. With every step he took, the floorboards creaked under his sturdy frame. It certainly wasn't a place he could creep up on anyone, and typically as he entered the kitchen, his wife immediately turned from her chair at the table well before he'd got anywhere near her.

Justine's face was one of stone. He couldn't remember the last time she'd smiled. Not that he could blame her. Times were tough and had only gotten worse when the conflict with the Arcadians broke out.

"How is it out there?" she asked.

Yevgeny stepped around to the other side of the table and pulled out a chair, dragging it along the floor and creating a piercing screech throughout the kitchen. "Do you really want to know?"

She waded through the data pads filling the table and tapped away at one in front of her. She slid it across to him, and he checked the figures.

He dropped his head. "Those rates have gone up."

Justine nodded. "Not to mention we got a fourth and final notice on the utilities."

"How are we going with an extension on the mortgage?"

His wife rifled through some of the pads and produced what she was looking for, handing it over to him. Yevgeny threw it down in disgust. He'd despised taking out a new mortgage on his land. But he'd had little choice. He could only imagine the four generations of Novikov before him rolling over in their graves.

"Is there any good news?" he asked.

"Good news?" She reached for another pad. "Well, Jana sent us some more money from her latest paycheck."

"She shouldn't be doing that."

"No, she shouldn't. But you know her. She cares about this place. And us." Justine collated all the pads into one neat pile. "Unfortunately, with the last crop being spoiled and the debt continuing to increase, the bank will likely take the ranch within the next four months."

Yevgeny peered past his wife through the window at the yellowness of their native sun baking the surrounding landscape. "Has to be in the hottest four months of the year, doesn't it?"

"We've got to make a decision, Yev. Neither of us are getting any younger, and it's not like we have Rik here to help us anymore. We can't afford to pay anyone else, so—"

"You're talking about selling up?"

"If we don't sell up, it'll be taken away."

Yevgeny stood and paced the length of the old kitchen the first Novikov settler had built over a hundred years earlier. "This is all I've known my whole life."

"It's all I've known my whole life, too, but it's got to the point where we can't do it anymore." His wife got to her feet and walked over to him, stopping him in his tracks. Her features softened, and she put a hand around his waist. "It's time, Yev."

Before he could utter a reply, an old horseshoe nailed to the wall flipped, and the kitchen floor shook. The pair knitted their brows, and Yevgeny led Justine onto the back porch. He grasped the wooden handrail, and the reverberation through the ground ran up his arm and rattled his bones. His wife pointed upward, and in the distance, several small specks filled the blue Gelbrana sky.

An unsettling pit formed in Yevgeny's stomach as the specks turned into larger shapes. Ones that were unmistakable for anything else. He'd never been a military man, but he watched the news. "Arcadians."

The crafts flew overhead, and a formation of bombers followed. Yevgeny took Justine by the hand, and they hurried to the other side of their house to follow the flight path of the invaders.

Justine squeezed him tight. "They're heading toward Hallopo!"

The troop ships peeled off, giving the bombers a clear shot at the small township nearest to their farm.

Then they fired.

Balls of destructive energy rained down over the horizon, and the sound of the structures crumbling filled the fields around them. The bombers eventually cleared off, and the troop ships zeroed in on the surface.

Yevgeny peeled Justine from him and grasped each of her shoulders. The woman did her best to stay strong, but she shook like a leaf just the same. Suddenly, all the worries of their previous conversation disappeared. Survival had taken on a new meaning.

"Justine, get my gun."

TWO

Logan could almost hear sleep calling out to him as his eyes wavered and his head bobbed.

Clip!

His eyes burst open. Then dropped again.

Clip!

Logan shook off his impending slumber and turned to the man sitting next to him in the copilot's seat of the craft which had been christened the *Corina II*. Not only were his colleague's boots off, but his socks had been tossed to the deck, too.

"Do you really need to do that in here?" Logan asked him.

Vernon clipped another of his yellowed toenails, and it disappeared somewhere beneath his seat. "No, but I don't much like the idea of you being in the cockpit on your own while fighting fatigue."

Logan rubbed his face and leaned over, grabbing his cup of coffee. It was cold, but he couldn't say no to caffeine. "We haven't come across an Arcadian patrol for days." He tapped his head. "Remember, James Sutter's up in here, and he's been able to plot a course around any major areas the Empire might be lurking."

"Just because we haven't seen any of them, doesn't mean they're not out here somewhere." Vernon finished with his right foot and moved on to the left. "To suggest otherwise is cocky. That's probably the part of the James Sutter you need to bury the most."

"Believe me, I would if I could." Logan checked over the scopes to ensure their course remained clear. Ever since they'd departed the Outer Rim, his thoughts usually wandered to Novikova, but the part of him that was James Sutter thought about his family, too. He still hadn't got used to the idea that he'd be forever two men melded together as one. He'd hoped their trip would have helped, but with such little to do until they reached their destination, the memories of the pair continued to swirl inside him.

Vernon completed his pedicure, returning the small space from a beauty parlor back into a cockpit. The old man raised his eyebrows at him obviously noticing something in his features. "What's going on inside that noodle of yours?"

Logan wished he could form the words to explain it to him. "I'm thinking I can't wait to get out of this tin can and stretch my legs. It's been too long being cooped up in here with you. No offense."

"You're as a much a pain in the ass as I am."

Logan chuckled. In the time they'd traveled together, they'd got more acquainted with one another than at any point since their first meeting on Telstar Station.

"It seems like you're about to get your wish." Vernon pointed at the scopes and put his boots back on. "We're approaching the Bolaran Star System."

Logan placed his hands on the controls and prepared to exit hyperwarp. "You haven't been here since *then*, have you?"

A darkness fell over the craggy lines of Vernon's face. "Just steer the ship."

Logan didn't follow up with another question. He knew all too well the signs of Vernon shutting himself off. Thankfully, the second Bolaran moon was fast approaching to break up any awkward silence. "Here we go." He pulled the vessel from hyperwarp, and the huge barren orb that was the smallest of Bolar's three satellites filled the viewport.

He put on the brakes, firing the forward thrusters to ensure they didn't career into the massive astral object. Gravity took hold, and he brought them into the moon's orbit. "What are the scopes telling you?"

Vernon tapped his fingers over the console in front of him. "Little now that we've hidden behind the moon, but for a split second just after leaving hyperwarp, it looked like the entire system was crawling with Arcadian bogeys."

"Seems the Empire's on their toes out here with the Bolarans giving them a bit of a bloody nose of late. That's got to be good news for us."

Vernon simply grunted without reply, keeping his eyes peeled on the scopes. "I wonder where they are?"

Logan peered over at the screens with no other discernable contacts within range. He suddenly felt very naked a long way from home. "This is where they told us to rendezvous, right?"

Vernon glowered out of the corner of his eye. Before a retort could come, his console beeped. A singular bogey appeared on the monitor, heading in their direction.

"That must be them," Logan said.

A second contact materialized. Then a third.

"I wouldn't count on it." Vernon cleared his throat. "Those are Arcadian fighters."

Logan checked to ensure his mentor wasn't losing his marbles. Sure enough, the IDs of the incoming crafts were identical to the vessels James Sutter made a name for himself in. "Could this have been a trap?"

"Not unless the Bolarans are working with the Arcadians." Vernon punched in a series of commands. "I think we just got extremely unlucky going headlong into the heart of this hornet's nest."

Logan fired the craft in the opposite direction to the incoming fighters. Where he was heading, he didn't know, but it had to be better than waiting for their imminent destruction from their more maneuverable and stronger counterparts. "It might be a good idea to arm our defenses."

"What does it look like I'm doing?" Vernon said, activating the ship's small arsenal. "We've got three missiles in the rear tubes and four in the front."

"Those four in the forward tubes will be useless. There's no chance we can take them head-on."

"If you just concentrate on steering this thing, hopefully we won't need them." Vernon activated the targeting computer. "Once I've got a lock on them—" His console beeped. "Dammit, that was quick! There's two missiles heading our way!"

Logan fought with the helm controls and broke out a sequence of evasive maneuvers. The first missile passed them, barely scraping the port wing. The second exploded off the starboard side. Space quaked around them, while Logan did his best to keep them on course. Vernon held his finger above the launch controls, waiting for a target.

The monitor finally flashed red, and he launched the first of their missiles.

It charged through space between them and their three pursuers, missing the first fighter, and the second.

But just as it was about to fizzle out, it made contact with the trailing craft. On the monitor, the bogey blinked out, leaving two Arcadians remaining.

"How the hell did you do that?" Logan asked him in astonishment.

"The moron was sitting too close behind the other fighters," Vernon told him, preparing to fire again. "He wouldn't have seen me coming and didn't have time to alter course. Arcadian cockiness at its best."

On the scopes, the other two fighters split up, breaking formation. They each fired another missile, and the projectiles blazed toward them. Logan took care of the first, barrel rolling from its path, but the second stayed with him.

Vernon fired again, launching the last missile from their rear tube. The Arcadian missile locked on to it, and they collided, exploding to the stern, lurching the ship ever so slightly from the shock wave.

"Thanks," Logan said. "But they're still closing. What I wouldn't give to be in a fighter right about now."

"We just have to use what's at our disposal." Vernon's tone remained calm. He focused on the targeting computer and got a lock. He fired, exhausting the last of the rear tubes.

The missile inched closer to the enemy while the incessant beeping of the computer confirmed it remained on course. Then the Arcadian fighter broke to port, narrowly avoiding destruction.

Logan sighed. He wasn't surprised, though. With the maneuverability of the Empire's best fighters, he and Vernon were on a hiding to nothing.

The cogs in the old man's mind seemed to turn, and he glanced sideways at Logan. "Slow down."

"Slow down?" Logan was about to ask if he was going

crazy, but a knowing look from Vernon put him on the same page. "Right. Got it." He slammed down hard on the thrusters, halting their forward momentum.

Both fighters flew by them, and Vernon quickly ran his hands over his controls. He fired three of the ship's forward missiles. The first went between the enemy contacts, the second missed the port-side craft by mere centimeters, but the third made contact with the one to starboard.

The projectile struck the rear thruster assembly, and the enemy pilot tried to pull up. The hit didn't look that that bad. Then the fighter exploded, lighting up the space in front of them.

"The last fighter's looping back around," Logan said. "How many missiles have we got left?"

"One." Vernon's finger hovered over the button. The targeting computer attempted to get a lock and finally blinked red.

He fired.

But nothing happened.

Logan craned his neck toward him. "What's going on?"

Vernon tried to fire again, but their lone missile refused to deploy.

A malfunction warning scrolled across the monitor, and Logan and Vernon stared at each other as the Arcadian continued on an intercept course.

THREE

"They're firing!"

Vernon's voice drifted somewhere into the background while Logan tried to move the hulk of the less maneuverable vessel out of danger. He was great pilot. A really great pilot. But even that arrogant ass inside him knew there was little he could do at such close quarters against a superior enemy.

He pulled the ship to starboard and rolled the craft as hard as she'd go. The g-forces were fierce, and the missile homing in on them continued unabated. There wasn't even time to say goodbye to the man beside him.

Then a bright flash filled the viewport.

"What the hell?"

Vernon leaned over his console. "The missile's been taken out."

Another blast erupted, much bigger than the first. The two men shielded their eyes from the glare, and they checked the scopes.

"The fighter's gone," Vernon said.

"Destroyed?"

"Yes. I'm picking up another bogey, though. It looks like the Bolarans have finally arrived."

"Not a moment too soon." Logan brought the ship back onto its proper axis and rendezvoused with the Bolaran fighter approaching their position. The smaller craft stopped off their bow, and the two vessels stared off with each other. Silence lingered inside the cockpit for several moments. "Are they hailing?"

"No." Vernon double-checked his console. "But they've still got their targeting computer activated."

"What the hell are they playing at?" Logan put his hand over the thruster control in case things turned nasty. "Maybe we should hail them."

Vernon did so, opening a channel. "Bolaran fighter. We're here at the consent of the Bolaran Rebellion. We request passage to our destination."

White noise was their only reply.

The fighter finally turned, and a voice came to life over the speakers. *"Passage has been granted. Deactivate your scopes and we'll escort you to the agreed destination."*

"The bastards just wanted to see us sweat." Logan locked in a course and got the ship moving. They went slowly to the moon's orbit and dived toward the surface. "If this is how they treat us up here, how will they treat us down there?"

The walk from the flight deck embedded deep in the rock of the moon was as excruciating as Vernon expected. Not only was the welcoming committee armed, their wary faces were filled with complete disdain of his and Logan's presence.

The group of thugs ushered them through the catacombs, where they passed more of the moon's inhabitants on their journey. They were members of the rebellion and civilians alike. There were even children. They were the only Bolarans who seemed to have an innocence about them. Vernon knew, however, it would only last for so long. Soon they'd be on the front line against the Empire, just like the rest of them.

"I feel like I'm being marched to my execution," Logan whispered.

"Who said you aren't?" Vernon said.

The younger man's mouth opened ever so slightly at the quip. Though in a way, it wasn't really a joke. Vernon had fought the Bolarans long ago and knew they were people not to be trifled with. Stories of their barbarity were commonplace back when he was a pilot for the Empire, and if what they'd seen was anything to go by, the propaganda might have held some truth.

The narrow catacombs widened and opened out into a vast space, not unlike a grand hall. Amongst it were more armed Bolarans. Some sat on scattered boulders, while others mingled between themselves around the outer walls. As Logan and Vernon entered, the conversations ended and everyone's attention turned to them.

The crowd moved aside at the opening on the far side of the hall, and two large men walked over to Vernon and Logan with rifles in their hands. Just as it seemed Logan was about to say something, one of them snarled at him.

Vernon put a hand on the young man's shoulder, ensuring the part of him that was James Sutter did nothing stupid. Through the opening, another figure emerged. She wasn't anywhere near as large or as ugly. If anything, she was quite beautiful, with piercing blue eyes, vivid red hair, and snow-white skin. If it wasn't for the scars on her muscular arms, Vernon would have sworn she was a porcelain doll.

She looked both men up and down with a face of

stone before spinning around and strolling to the far wall, perching herself on one of the boulders like it was her throne. Vernon took the lead, and Logan followed, stopping before her, wary of the guards remaining on either side of them.

"I'm Alira, leader of the Bolaran Rebellion," the woman said, breaking her silence. "It's not often we get visitors to Bolar. At least not those who aren't soldiers of the Empire. I understand you ran into some trouble on the way here."

"Thankfully, you showed up when you did." Vernon took out his hands in an open manner. "If you hadn't, we might not have made it."

"You did well to destroy two of the Arcadians' fighters. You couldn't quite get the job done against the third one, though. I would've expected more of the great Charles Vernon and James Sutter."

Laughs rang out around the hall.

Vernon's colleague appeared jittery beside him, but the part of him that was Logan seemed to be doing a good job at keeping Sutter buried inside him. "Our reputations precede us then."

"Well, of course. You're infamous among my people. Charles Vernon was a part of the invasion force which brought the rule of the Empire to Bolar. His piloting exploits are common knowledge." Alira cast her gaze across to Logan. "And James Sutter... While he might've built his reputation in the Outer Rim, he also had time to visit Bolar more than once to put down our continued attempts at regaining our freedom. Naturally, we've heard about the Empire's scheme to implant his memories into another man. Is it really true? Does Sutter live inside there?"

Logan nodded. "A part of him. But I'm not Sutter anymore. I'm Nathan Logan."

She seemed unconvinced and crossed her arms, returning her attention to Vernon. "You've come a long way. What could possibly have brought you here?"

Vernon coughed, pushing aside the dryness in his throat. "I'm here representing the Outer Rim Coalition to relay a message."

"And that message is?"

"We come to seek an alliance."

Everyone in the hall broke out into raucous laughter. All except Alira. Vernon held a steely gaze with her until she finally glared at her people to bring silence back to the catacombs.

"An alliance?" she scoffed. "Between Bolar and the Rim?"

Vernon straightened his back, as much as he could in his old age. "I fail to see what's so unbelievable about that."

"Really?" Alira stood. "Those in the Outer Rim are nothing but the scraps of the Empire. Until recently, you considered yourselves Arcadians. Generations of your people helped perpetrate the Empire's atrocities by expanding their borders until it encompassed all of humanity. To ask for help after everything you've done..."

Vernon stepped closer to her, and the guards moved with him. "I'm not here to apologize for my sins, or those of my people. I know the wrong I did, but times have changed. We've got a common enemy. If we don't band together, we'll never be able to bring an end to the Empire's tyranny."

The woman peered out at her people, and they stared back at her expectantly. "What you ask is impossible. Too much blood has been spilled."

"And more will be spilled if we don't do something about it. If we can't come to some form of understanding,

23

you'll consign everyone who is within the emperor's grasp to oppression forever."

"Kolar!"

Vernon spun around to a single voice among the Bolarans. It was only one man somewhere at the back, but the word was crystal clear.

More spoke the same word until it broke out into a deafening chant throughout the hall. "Kolar! Kolar! Kolar!"

"What are they saying?" Logan asked.

"They're calling us puppets in Bolaran," Vernon said. "They believe we're the pawns of the Empire."

Alira stood back and motioned at the guards. They grabbed Vernon and Logan by the arms and dragged them from the hall. The bloodcurdling cries of the Bolarans echoed all the way down the catacombs and into their cells.

FOUR

Jana Novikova was aware how hot it could get on Gelbrana, but the fires still burning across the planet were making the air thicker and dirtier, ratcheting the temperature to a near unbearable level. It was so bad, in fact, that the dark clouds above were blocking out the beautiful blue sky and creating a greenhouse effect that would likely bake the colony for weeks if not months to come.

As she sat in the passenger seat of the speeder, she carried a hopelessness along with her, one she'd felt since they'd received word aboard the *Ringwood* of the attack launched on Gelbrana by Arcadian forces. She couldn't forget the blank look on Captain Estrada's face when he'd told her the news. The shock of it had hit her all at once, followed by concern for her parents. With no way to communicate with the colony, sadness soon turned to anger.

Estrada, being the big old softy he was, altered course when it appeared the Arcadians had left Gelbrana. They'd joined many humanitarian convoys and arrived in orbit to find an apocalyptic level of waste laid on her home world. She'd seen nothing like it. There'd always been stories about the ruthlessness of Arcadian soldiers, but the state she'd found the colony exceeded anything she'd ever expected. Not only were the humble cities of the farming planet leveled, but the satellite towns linking the regions had also been turned to rubble. There wasn't a patch of dirt anywhere that hadn't been scorched.

Normally when the Empire moved into their enemy's territory, they'd seize a foothold to gain advantage and launch more attacks. But with Gelbrana, they'd gone through like a tornado and left the planet in their wake.

"Is this what we've got to look forward to?"

Captain Estrada, who hadn't said a word since arriving on the surface, glanced at her out the corner of his eye, while steering the speeder across the famous Gelbrana plains. "Sorry, what was that, Nova?"

"The Empire. They've taken a new tack." She leaned her arm on the door of the speeder. "The Rim's been a thorn in their side long enough. This is a message. Either submit or we'll burn you to the ground."

The skipper didn't immediately answer, adjusting course around some smoking bushes. "I doubt they would've taken the ORC's reply to the emperor's pleas for surrender too well."

"It had to be this colony they made an example of, didn't it?" She pointed ahead at the smoldering crops. "It's over there."

Estrada continued on and drove the speeder through a broken fence and past what remained of the corn crops slashed to the ground. More plumes of smoke appeared, and Novikova sat higher in her seat. A tear welled in her eye, and Estrada took her hand. He slowed and pulled the vehicle up at the front of the ranch house.

At least what was left of it.

Novikova swung the door open and hopped out of the speeder. The house was never extravagant, but it held the memories of a childhood she'd never get back. Estrada stood well behind her while she walked to the front porch.

It was burned to a crisp, just like the rest of the house. All that remained of the old dwelling was the chimney, which only ever got a few days of use during the winter months. Memories flooded back to her, and she gazed across at where the rooms once stood. From the kitchen, to the living area, to her room. It was all gone.

She tiptoed through the debris, careful not to step onto anything that might give way, until she found herself in the heart of the house. Everything was so charred that barely any of it was recognizable. She was about to continue, but something stared up at her with a familiar shape. She kneeled and grasped it in her hand, rubbing the ash from it.

"Dad's lucky horseshoe," she whispered.

More tears ran down her cheeks, and she turned, spotting something else. The legs had fallen off, and it was black like the rest of the debris, but the ovular kitchen table was unmistakable. She moved closer to it, remembering the countless meals she'd had sitting at the rickety old thing. She bent down and reached toward it. Then a hand grabbed her from behind, bringing her to a halt.

Novikova spun around to find Estrada with a vigorous grip on her. She looked back at the table and spotted two burned pairs of legs underneath the wooden slab.

"Let's go, Nova," he said to her.

She wanted to let out all her rage. She wanted all her tears to flood out. The skipper tried to pull her back, but she wouldn't budge.

A cacophony of noise blasted over the top of them, and a small transport vessel appeared in the sky. It maneuvered downward and landed on the other side of the ranch house. Novikova finally gave in and allowed Estrada to help her through what remained of her childhood home, back onto solid ground. The ramp to the transport opened, and a group of ORC soldiers marched down it. They spread out to examine the carnage left behind by the Arcadians, while an officer stopped at the bottom of the ramp.

He examined the pile of ashes and shifted his gaze to Novikova and Estrada. "I'm searching for…" He double-checked his data pad. "…Yevgeny Novikov and Justine Novikova."

Novikova couldn't spit out a reply. Estrada gave the officer a knowing look, and it appeared the man understood immediately what he was getting at.

"Have you found any survivors?" Estrada asked him.

"Not many. It would seem the Arcadians had only one aim here…" The ORC man stopped himself mid-sentence, returning his attention to Novikova. "I'm sorry for your loss." He gestured to the rest of his soldiers, and they went back to the transport, hurrying up the ramp. He went to join them, but Novikova clutched his arm.

"Where are they now?" she asked him.

"I'm not sure I understand," the officer said.

"The Arcadians. The ones who did this. Where are they?"

He removed her hand as delicately as he could. "They're pushing farther into the Rim. Our forces are preparing to go on the counterattack."

Novikova studied Estrada's solemn features, and she stepped closer to the officer. "Where do you think you're going without me?"

FIVE

The view of the war games from Admiral Jones's office was perfect. Not only could he see the entire battlefield in orbit above Malala VI, but also every ship and fighter clearly taking part in the exercise. He turned his head slightly to have a closer look at the holographic projection above his desk, relaying all the relevant data from the games, and how each vessel in the advanced simulation was faring.

At the end of the day, though, he was only interested in a few of the pilots taking part. He had to go back several years the last time he'd seen such artistry behind the controls of a fighter. It was déjà vu on a whole other level. For a single pilot to have such a natural ability was one thing, but for five was quite another. It was as if they could read each other's thoughts and anticipate one another's moves.

"Bridge to Admiral," a voice from a junior officer on the *Imperator's* bridge called over the intercom.

Jones reached through the hologram to activate the intercom on top of his desk. "This is Jones. Go ahead."

"Sir, we're receiving a transmission from the Emperor's Council. It's Councilor McCrae."

Jones sighed. It wasn't that he didn't have the time for

his superior; he wouldn't be in the position he was without the man's support. But some days he preferred the rawness of dealing with the war at the coalface. Getting involved in the politics of the Empire was even dirtier work and much more unsavory. "Send the transmission down here."

"Yes, sir," replied the junior officer.

The hologram of the war games disappeared, and on the other side of the admiral's desk, a holographic projection of Councilor McCrae emerged from the shadows. Not a moment went by when the man didn't look like Father Time had robbed him of his life expectancy. It could have been as subtle as a few more gray hairs, or an extra wrinkle on his forehead, but especially of late, the heaviness of McCrae's eyes was telling. Jones could only imagine the toll the conflict was taking on those serving the emperor in the council chambers. It was said the emperor's temper could be worse than an entire fleet's arsenal.

Jones nodded respectfully. "Councilor McCrae."

"Jones." His older superior barely grunted his greeting. *"How are the war games proceeding?"*

"Everything is going to plan."

"And our new pilots?"

"It's too early to tell, but I've been impressed with their initial maneuvers."

"Good." McCrae's hologram stepped closer to the desk. *"And what have you got to report from the front?"*

Jones sat and dived into the top drawer, pulling out a cigar. He placed it in his mouth and lit it with his favorite lighter. "After the destruction of Gelbrana, the rebels went on the counterattack as we pushed farther into the Rim. While we did damage to their forces, we had no choice but to regroup."

"As was my prediction."

"The closer we move into the Outer Rim, the more concentrated the enemy's forces will be. We grossly outmatch them, but we must be smart about it. It won't take long for reinforcements to arrive, and we'll be able to once again go on the attack." Jones noted the ever so slight grin at the corner of the councilor's mouth. "Has the emperor decided whether to offer the rebels a chance to surrender again?"

McCrae shook his head. *"There will be no further offers. The Outer Rim Coalition has made its bed. Now they must lie in it."*

Jones swiveled the cigar in his fingers. From the day the ORC had decided to fight the Empire, he knew he'd have to engage old friends who'd taken up arms against their fellow Arcadians. He'd come across many in battle and sent a lot to their graves. Sometimes he couldn't help but feel guilty, but then he remembered he was a man of war and that he was simply dispatching traitors to the afterlife. "I'll continue do everything in my power to bring a swift end to the rebellion."

"See that you do." The image of the councilor disappeared and was promptly replaced with the war game's projection.

Jones leaned over and raised his eyebrows at the results before him. He hit the intercom with his spare hand. "Jones to bridge."

"Go ahead, sir," came the same voice from earlier.

"Tell, Doctor Vanstrom I'd like to see her."

"Aye, Admiral."

It didn't take long for the new head of Artemis Unit to arrive. The doors slid open at the far end of his office, and the youthful doctor strode in. She had an air of confidence about her that was quite contagious. It was a nice change compared to the pathetic figure of the late Doctor Agata.

"You wanted to see me, Admiral," she said, placing her hands together in front of her.

"Have you been keeping up to date with the war games?" he asked.

"I have."

"Did you believe they'd be this good?"

She walked closer to the desk and examined the results coming in from the simulation. "Project Caravale has been under my purview for some time, Admiral. I predicted nothing less than you're seeing here."

Jones stroked his chin as the squadron of pilots with James Sutter's implanted memories cut a swathe through the other Arcadians' vessels, roleplaying as ORC contacts. The Sutter he remembered from the day he'd left the Fighter Corps Academy was as close to perfection as he'd ever seen. To witness it five-fold with a small squadron was something else entirely. "You've done tremendous work here, Doctor." He took a puff of his cigar, and the smoke wafted through the hologram. "I'm going to send these pilots to the front. How many more can you give to me to sign off?"

"There are fifty-four more ready to go here on the *Imperator*," she informed him. "I can have another eighty transported here for testing within the week."

"Good. With any luck this war will be over soon, and no matter how canny the ORC's leadership is, we'll overwhelm them with a fleet of Red Hawks." He turned in his chair and stared through the viewport at Doctor Vanstrom's handiwork. In the reflection, there was a determination in the woman's eyes. Her attitude was exactly what Artemis needed. And also what the war needed.

Fresh blood...

As he continued looking out at the games, for a moment he recalled the first campaign James Sutter flew. His movements were so pure. His confidence so arrogant. His skill so complete. To this day, Jones hadn't been able to forgive himself for losing the man to the ORC. The fact that he was still out in the guise of another person burned him to his core. He'd tried to push the memories of Sutter aside in the past weeks but failed spectacularly. Jones didn't know whether he was getting too soft in his old age or just feeble.

He swiveled back around to the expectant face of Doctor Vanstrom. "I don't suppose you've got anything to report from that other little assignment I had you investigate, have you?"

SIX

"What's your name?"

Logan stared at the interrogator on the other side of the table as the deep-brown eyes of the man gazed across at him. From the moment he'd been dragged into the small smelly room, containing a single table, a pair of chairs, and a dodgy ceiling light, the Bolaran had remained aloof. He'd instructed Logan to put his hand on the Kowalski Machine between them and rifled question after question at him. After what seemed like hours of going back and forth, he was beginning to tire of the pointless exercise.

"You've already asked me that," Logan told him.

"Did I?" The interrogator's face remained frozen of emotion. "Please, answer it again."

"Surely by now you've got all you're going to get from me."

"While Kowalski Machines are incredibly accurate, they're not infallible. Charles Vernon can attest to that during your first meeting together."

Logan crossed his arms, recalling the many times his interrogator had left the room before returning. "You've been exchanging notes. You've got Vernon hooked up to one of these things in another room, don't you?"

The Bolaran didn't answer, instead pointing at the Kowalski Machine. "Please place your hand back on the device."

Logan ground his teeth and gave in, doing as he was instructed. The machine produced a blue light between them, bathing the tiny space in an eerie glow.

"Now tell me again, what's your name?"

Vernon coughed, covering his mouth with the other hand from the one sitting atop the Kowalski Machine. He couldn't remember the last time he'd gone through such an ordeal. Even the interrogation by the ORC leadership after their rescue from the Olarus Nebula hadn't been as thorough.

A lot of the questions asked were about his past and his relationship with Logan. He answered everything truthfully. He had no choice. Whatever lie he produced would be picked up by the device, regardless. And he hadn't come all the way to Bolar to prove their suspicions about them were correct. However, the questioning wasn't what he'd expected. He'd have thought his captors would have pressed more about the secrets of the ORC considering his high rank, but they'd asked nothing that would compromise him.

The interrogator switched off the Kowalski Machine, and the blue light extinguished. "That will be all for today."

"Does that mean I have to come back again?"

The interrogator didn't reply, placing the device in a case and standing, gesturing toward the door. Vernon didn't need to be told twice and heaved himself from his chair.

There, waiting for him in the corridor, looking almost as fatigued as he felt, was Logan. "How'd you go?" the young pilot asked him.

The guards motioned them forward, and they set off down the catacombs of the secret Bolaran moon base. "At least it was a little more pleasant than the cell they've held us in for the past two days. What about you? What did they ask?"

They rounded a corner, passing by some small children playing in a hole in the side of the excavated wall. "Funnily enough, similar questions to the ones you asked me when we first met."

Vernon nodded. "Seems like they were trying to get a baseline for you. They want to know you are who you claim to be."

"You think they fear I'm an Arcadian agent?"

"Of course. But if my questioning was anything to go by, I believe there's more to it than that." Vernon scratched his chin, spotting the detention section of the base ahead of them. "I shouldn't have expected anything less. The Bolarans were always notorious for toying with their prisoners. The stories I heard during the Empire's war with them were the thing of legend."

"What do you think they're going to do with us?"

"I don't have the faintest idea."

They arrived at the detention section, and the guards ushered them through the low ceiling of the entrance. Vernon and Logan stopped at the sight before them. They looked at each other for a moment and then at the woman standing in the middle of their cell.

With a data pad in one hand, a pistol in the other, Alira nodded at her guards. They shoved Vernon and Logan inside with her and disappeared around the corner, leaving the three of them alone. "Take a seat."

Vernon hesitated for a second but eventually sat on the wooden slab he'd attempted to sleep on for the last two nights. Logan did the same on the other side of the cell.

She held her gun up. "I won't need this, will I?"

Vernon shook his head.

Alira put the weapon in her holster and stepped toward the washbasin in the corner of their small jail where two glasses sat next to the tap. She filled them with water and gave one to each of the men. Vernon stared at his warily.

"I assure you, if I wanted to kill you, I wouldn't do it in such a cowardly manner," Alira said.

Vernon took a drink and quickly guzzled it all down, refreshing his parched throat from all the talking he'd done during his interrogation. He handed it back to her, and she took it, collecting the other glass from Logan and returning them to the washbasin.

She stood back between them. "You're probably both wondering what I'm doing here?"

Vernon wriggled on the bed, getting as comfortable as possible. "The last time we saw you, it seemed you were going to send us to the bottom of a hole to rot."

"Yes, well, that was a bit of theatre. As leader of the rebellion, it's expected of me to give the people what they want." She paced the cell from one end to the other. "You're Arcadians, even if you are from the Rim. There are many Bolarans still alive from the day the Empire invaded our home. To put it bluntly, no one here likes you, and for me to instill some kind of trust in you would've been a mistake."

"So, you're only in control of the masses, until you're not?"

"Something like that."

"Since you're in here with us, does that mean you trust us?" Logan asked.

"Not in the slightest." Alira chortled. "While you may not be soldiers of the Empire, you're still James Sutter and Charles Vernon. However..." She took a seat on the other end of Vernon's bed, and her features softened. "I watched you both being questioned, and I was satisfied with what I saw. So, let's say I would be prepared to entertain an alliance. I might even be able to convince the Thandeeans to help, too. But..."

"It'll come at a cost?"

"A cost. A condition. Proof that you're willing to form a true alliance. Call it what you will. It's a necessity if we're to go forward."

"What do you need?" Vernon asked.

"I have a confession to make. I'm not actually the leader of the Bolaran Rebellion." Alira got to her feet and walked over to the washbasin, leaning against its edge. "I'm simply keeping the seat warm. Our real leader's been captured, and you're going to help me set him free."

SEVEN

Logan and Vernon's eyes met at Alira's revelation, but their gaze quickly returned to the Bolaran woman standing before them.

"So, he's been captured by the Empire?" Logan assumed.

She nodded. "Keller left here two weeks ago on a mission to the core worlds of the Arcadian Empire."

"The core worlds?" Vernon raised his eyebrows. "From all the way out here? Did he have a death wish?"

Alira chuckled dryly. "More than you could know."

"What was his objective?"

"He didn't say."

"You're telling me the leader of the Bolaran Rebellion up and left to the heart of the Empire without telling his closest confidante what his intentions were?" Vernon stood and walked over to Alira, filling up another glass of water. "I find that extraordinary."

"You don't know him."

"No, I suppose I don't."

"What makes you believe he's still alive?" Logan asked.

"We aren't the backwater barbarians you think we are.

Let's just say we have a way of finding these things out," Alira assured him.

"Where is he?"

"We've tracked him to the Hestan Star System."

Vernon finished drinking from the glass and placed it back down. "Hestan? There's nothing in the Hestan Star System."

"That's not entirely true," Logan blurted out, not realizing he'd made the comment until after he'd said it.

The pair at the washbasin looked at him. None more quizzically than his older colleague.

"Well, spit it out, Logan," he told him.

"The Hestan Star System's home to a detention facility."

"Where? It contains six gas giants. Unless—"

"There's a station on the surface of an asteroid between the second and third planets."

Vernon went to the end of the bed. "This is the James Sutter inside you who knows that, right?"

"Sutter once visited the facility." Logan turned his attention to Alira. "Are you sure he's alive? Those who go to Hestan rarely come back out. He's likely been taken there for interrogation. Normally once the Arcadians are done with their prisoners, they're executed."

"Keller's still alive. He's unlikely to break, no matter what the Arcadians throw at him or inject into his veins." Before Logan could ask what she meant by the comment, Alira continued. "With that said, he's not invincible. Eventually, their methods will kill him. That's why it's imperative to get him out of there before that happens."

Logan couldn't help but notice the pain in her voice. The man obviously meant a lot to the rebellion. The bravado she exuded with the other Bolarans around here had all but disappeared. "No one has ever escaped from Hestan."

"Why do you think I'm asking for your assistance?"

Logan and Vernon again exchanged a wary glance.

"I don't know what you think we can do," Logan told her. "Just because I've visited the facility once, doesn't mean I can stroll in there and rescue him."

"Perhaps not. But deep down you're still the Red Hawk." Alira faced Vernon. "And while you're a frail shadow of the man who invaded my homeland, your infamy still lives large. Let's not forget you both took down Artemis Unit by going behind enemy lines. You have a knack for achieving the impossible." She picked the glasses from the washbasin. "Besides, as I said earlier, you either help me or there's no chance of an alliance between our peoples."

"If we somehow pull this off, what's stopping you from going back on your word?" Vernon asked as she stepped toward the door of the cell.

Alira swung it open and leaned on the handle. "You'll just have to trust me, won't you?"

She departed and locked the door behind her, disappearing into the shadows of the catacombs beyond the detention section. The two men stared at each other for several moments until Logan went to speak. Vernon, though, beat him to it.

"When was the last time you visited Hestan?"

Logan had to delve into the mind that still percolated with the memories of James Sutter. While he'd recovered most of them from his time as the Red Hawk, not a day went by when more emerged, slowly completing the puzzle. "It's been a few years now."

"Let's hope Sutter's memory doesn't let us down."

"So, does that mean we're really doing this?"

Vernon sighed. "It's either that or get comfortable in Hotel Bolar."

———

The view from the bridge of the *Ringwood* was almost hypnotic as it shot across the stars at hyperwarp. Novikova touched one of the rear workstations, and the vibration of the thirty-year-old engine ran through her bones. She'd spent a long time working on the worn-out ore transport, but she could take solace in the fact she'd be leaving it in better shape than she'd found it. She had to find solace in something, even if it was something so trivial.

"We're approaching the rendezvous," Jed Grayson called out from the helm.

"Take us to sub-light," the pacing Estrada instructed him from the center of the bridge.

The streaking stars disappeared and were replaced with the points of light of faraway constellations. Once upon a time, Novikova dreamed about the stories each one held and the infinite possibilities they represented. Now she didn't care.

Just ahead of the *Ringwood* the Outer Rim fleet took shape, consisting of carriers, cruisers, destroyers, and everything in between. The skipper slowly made his way toward her.

"Are you sure about this?" he asked.

She didn't answer him.

"Can I at least escort you to the airlock?"

She nodded and picked up the bags containing her belongings. They departed the bridge and headed to the launch bay at the rear of the ship. Estrada had said little to her since they'd left Gelbrana. She wasn't sure whether it was because he knew she didn't want to talk about it or because he didn't know what to say.

They passed several of the ship's crew on the way, and those she'd come to know in her time aboard the vessel either nodded their goodbye or ran up and gave her a hug. Returning their embraces were difficult. It was as if she'd left all her strength on Gelbrana.

Estrada led her around the corner, and they finally reached the airlock. He tapped on the control panel, but stopped before opening it. His hulking presence blocked Novikova's path, and he looked at her with his deep, dark eyes. "I can't let you go without asking you one more time. Is this what you really want?"

"You'll find another engineer," she said.

"This isn't about me," he scoffed. "Once you step through that airlock, there's no coming back."

"I understand that."

"Do you?"

"Only a few days ago I landed on the surface of my home world to find my parents dead, so yeah, I know what I'm getting myself into. If it wasn't for them, I would have done this when the rebellion started. Now that they're gone..."

Novikova drifted off, and the skipper moved closer to her, putting his large mitts on her shoulders. All she wanted to do was cry, but she couldn't. "It's all hands on deck now. We either fight them with everything we've got, or they'll burn it all to the ground."

Estrada closed his eyes and bowed his head. "You've been a hell of a find, Nova. I'm not sure what I would've done without out you. The *Ringwood* won't ever be the same."

She wrapped her arms around the man, and he squeezed her tight. "It's not too late to come with me."

Estrada laughed for a moment and let her go. He stepped aside and opened the airlock. He did his best impersonation of a soldier saluting, and she did the same. "Goodbye, Nova."

She walked over the threshold and entered the darkness.

EIGHT

It was quiet on the *Corina II*. More so than Logan thought possible with the amount of Bolarans crammed into it. He cracked his knuckles and shifted in his seat. His thoughts drifted to Novikova somewhere on the *Ringwood*.

He wondered if he'd ever see her again.

"Are you ready?"

In the viewport's reflection, Logan spotted Vernon enter from the rear of the cockpit.

"Is it that time already?" Logan asked.

"Put the ship on auto. We've got an appointment to keep."

Logan locked down the helm and followed Vernon into the rear compartment where Alira and the team of Bolaran soldiers she'd brought with her were milling around. While the petite woman was a formidable force all on her own, the other six men dwarfed their leader by some margin. They were strong, battle-hardened, and arrogant. Logan knew how handy they'd be going up against the finest the Empire had to throw at them, but he could have done without the bravado.

Alira noticed Logan and Vernon entering, and she glared at her men to get themselves in order. They looked at her and then at their two hosts, who took seats at the head of the table. The soldiers dispensed with the mugs of coffee they were drinking, and their conversations came to a standstill. Instead of sitting, they decided to loiter around the edge of the humble kitchen space.

Logan felt every eyeball in the room on him, especially Alira's, who took a position opposite him. He was used to being the center of attention, but he couldn't help but feel the Bolarans were fantasizing of all the different ways they could kill him. Pushing aside the grizzly thoughts, he pressed a panel in front of him, and the lights dimmed. A hologram materialized above the table with a single point of light.

"This is the Hestan Star System." He raised a hand and waved at the projection, zooming in and revealing the six planets of the system—all gas giants. He zoomed in again between the second and third planets, where an asteroid field appeared. "And this is our target."

He pushed in closer, allowing everyone a better view at the detention facility built into the surface of one of the larger asteroids.

"Why is it that your people are so obsessed with building their strongholds inside the middle of asteroid fields?" a Bolaran soldier asked beyond the holographic projection.

Logan didn't know all their names yet, but the distinct guttural tone of Briggs was hard to miss. The man was no doubt throwing out some bait for either him or Vernon to nibble on. "It probably has something to do with the fact they're a navigational nightmare," Logan said as diplomatically as possible. "Unless you're well-versed with the geography and a skilled pilot, you likely won't make it through."

"Isn't it lucky that we have the great James Sutter with

us then," Briggs spat. "For a minute I was worried we'd need the old man to take the controls."

"Enough!"

This time, the voice came from the other end of the table from the only female in the room. The soldier immediately shut his trap at Alira's command. "Continue, Logan."

Logan glanced at Vernon, whose demeanor told him to get on with it. He did so and zoomed out, returning to the image. "Unfortunately, the asteroid field's only one of our barriers. The hardest section to navigate will be the star system's scope network."

Several dots appeared throughout the system. Colored spheres burst out from each, revealing the range of the scope buoys.

Alira leaned in toward the hologram. "I don't see many gaps in that."

Logan nodded. "That's because there aren't many. Certainly not enough for us to reach the asteroid field undetected."

"So, what can we do to get through it?"

"That's where we have to rely on some luck." Logan turned to Vernon, who took the baton from him and continued the briefing.

"The Hestan Star System uses a Type-J scope network," he said. "They were new when I left the Fighter Corps and were quite advanced for their time. However, they do have one big flaw."

"And what's that?" Alira asked.

"The buoys near the sun have a tendency to be defective depending on its orbit during certain solar cycles. At the moment the Hestan star's experiencing a moderate amount of activity. This means it's possible to move through certain sections undetected."

Logan deactivated all the holographic buoys around the sun and produced a line from the outside of the star system to the asteroid field. "As you can see, we have a path through, but we'll have to go in unpowered and use our thrusters sparingly. Even then, there's no guarantee it'll work."

Alira stared at him through the hologram. "If we get to the asteroid field, what's our next move?"

"Then we make a run at the detention facility. They have very few defenses. We should be able to take out their shield generator and then bombard them with the arsenal you've so kindly provided us. Then I hand the mission over to you, and your men to go down there and find Keller."

Silence permeated around the room for several moments. Even the Bolaran soldiers didn't say a word. They must have understood how ridiculous the plan was and how many risks they'd have to take.

The Bolaran woman finally stood. "Very well."

Logan deactivated the hologram and bathed the group in light. Alira departed first, heading to her quarters while the soldiers filed out after her. All except Briggs. Logan and Vernon got up and went to exit, but the soldier approached, towering over the two men.

"My grandfather died in the first attack on Bolar forty years ago." He stared at Vernon and then turned to Logan. "And my brother was shot down in a firefight with an Arcadian squadron a few months back."

The hulking beast brushed past them and down the corridor.

Logan shook his head. "If you need me, I'll be in the cockpit, polishing my gun."

NINE

"Get in line!"

Novikova followed the instructions of the officer at the door and moved into the enormous flight deck of the ORC carrier *Liberty Cry*. Inside, at least one thousand other recruits were lined up in rows. Some were survivors of the Gelbrana massacre, while others had traveled from all over the Rim to put up their hand for the cause. None were in uniform yet, instead in the civilian attire they'd worn from their various colonies. Some were farmers, others factory workers and miners. They did, however, have one thing in common, and that was the blue armbands with an individual six-digit number on it that they'd all been given after testing.

She couldn't remember the last time she'd seen so many people in one place. The *Ringwood*, though a large ship, only ever had one hundred and twenty crewmen on it at any one time.

"Move!" another officer yelled.

Novikova quickly upped her pace and followed the officer to the farthest bulkhead, where they stopped. She turned with the others and faced toward the inner wall where crew members of the *Liberty Cry* milled about.

More of her compatriots entered behind her and filled out the rest of the flight deck. By the end, there were over two thousand people from all over the Rim lined up and ready to join the rebellion.

Some quiet murmurs pervaded throughout. All except behind Novikova, where three men, all slightly younger than her, and attired in grubby mining fatigues, joked around with each other. She wondered if they truly knew what they were getting themselves into. One caught her gaze, and the three of them stopped and stared at her.

"What are you looking at, honey?" the one in the middle said to her, trying to impress his friends.

Novikova simply shook her head, and the trio sniggered behind her back.

Jackasses.

Eventually, the last of the murmurs subsided, and even the idiots behind her quietened down. The officers moved aside at the front of the flight deck, and another officer, slightly older than the rest, entered the vast section. She had short blonde hair and a lithe figure. While there were wrinkles and obvious fatigue on her face, she exuded confidence and demanded attention with her presence.

"Welcome," she said, her voice echoing off the tall bulkheads. "My name is Admiral Buckley. I'm the commanding officer of the Second Fleet. Once upon a time, someone in my position would have promised you the adventure of a lifetime. I'm not here to sugarcoat anything. Since I took over the command of this fleet, we've seen several victories. We've also seen our fair share of defeats. We've given many Arcadians a bloody nose, but we've lost many close to us. I'm sorry if this isn't the rousing speech you expected, but I want you all to understand what awaits you out there."

Someone coughed a few rows behind Novikova, and

the admiral continued. "We've all experienced hard lives in the Rim. As I look out at you, I see those from every walk of life. Being up here will take a certain resilience. Our enemy are trained and battle-hardened. They live for exactly the kind of conflict we're fighting. But we have something they don't. And that's something to fight for. I can see several Gelbranans with us today. My thoughts are with all of you right now. I know what you've lost, but I also realize that if you didn't believe there was still a cause to fight for you wouldn't be here with the rest of us."

Novikova's mind drifted to the smoldering house she'd grown up in.

"I understand you'll be hurting," the admiral said. "I understand you'll be angry. Keep those emotions close to you. I assure you the time will come when you'll be able to use them against our enemy. As for the rest of you, the Empire has shown us what they're capable of. At what lengths they're willing to go to defeat us. We're here to make sure that doesn't happen."

Dead silence filled the flight deck. Novikova glanced at the three jokers behind her. Even they were hanging on Buckley's every word.

"I don't say this to scare you. I say it because it's the reality of the situation we face." The admiral stepped closer to the front row of recruits, eying every one of them. "This is survival, pure and simple. We can either cower or fight. Now it's time to make your final decision. If you don't believe you have what it takes to serve, you're welcome to leave now. No one will think any less of you."

Slight rumblings broke out throughout the flight deck, and people whispered amongst themselves with those near them. Not a single person took Buckley's invitation. No one would have dared.

A smile rose on the admiral's harsh exterior, and one

of her offsiders gave her a data pad. "You've all been assigned to ships within the Second Fleet. Your overseeing officer will inform you of your posting and orders. You're to take what belongings you have and immediately report aboard your assignments. She handed the data pad back and placed her hands on her hips. "Welcome to the rebellion, ladies and gentlemen."

Buckley turned on her heel and departed the flight deck with the rest of her entourage. Conversations broke out as soon as she left, and the frenzy of activity commenced.

The officer beside Novikova pulled out a small device and scanned her armband. He checked the screen on it and pointed to another part of the bay. "You've been assigned to the *Defender*. Report to Pod-Eighteen. Move!"

Startled, she made sure her bag was over her shoulder and hurried off, trying not to get bowled over in all the commotion around her. She eventually found Pod-Eighteen and queued up at the ramp. One by one, those ahead of her had their armbands scanned again and were ushered aboard. Novikova stopped and had hers re-scanned, too. The officer nodded at her and pointed up the ramp. Just as it seemed she was the last of the recruits for the *Defender*, three more arrived. She rolled her eyes at the trio she recognized as the jackasses from earlier.

Great...

TEN

"You've been impressive since arriving here, Mister Sutter. These results are quite the achievement."

Sutter nodded his thanks at the Arcadian Fighter Corps Academy's commandant. He zipped up his jacket, doing his best to prevent a chill from his foreign surroundings, and the pair continued their walk of the vast lawns. Having been raised on Dylaria, he'd gotten used to the beautiful summers his home world had to offer but hadn't quite become accustomed yet to the briskness the native Arcadians enjoyed on their own planet. He didn't really understand why they preferred the fall-like conditions. With all the weather control systems throughout the atmosphere, they could change the planet's temperature with the flip of a switch.

Perhaps the emperor doesn't enjoy the heat...

"There's someone I'd like you to meet." Commandant Brown gestured at a man ahead of them in an admiral's uniform. The senior officer had a ramrod-straight back, several streaks of gray hair, and a set of unwavering eyes. "This is Admiral Jones—Commanding Officer of the Arcadian Third Fleet."

They stopped in front of him, and Sutter saluted,

trying to straighten his back as much as his superior's. "Admiral."

"At ease, Cadet," Jones instructed him.

Sutter relaxed his stance ever so slightly while the pair of older men exchanged pleasantries and shook hands. He did his best not to eavesdrop but found it difficult with them standing so close. They weren't, however, spilling any state secrets, instead it was little more than a few war buddies reminiscing about the past.

They said their farewells, and the commandant walked off in the other direction. Jones glanced at Sutter and waved down the path between the two main dormitories. Sutter strolled by the admiral's side and rubbed his cold hands together.

"Admiral Brown and I go a long way back. Not only did we graduate in the same class here, many years ago, but we also flew against the Thandeeans when we brought them under the emperor's rule. I still remember the conflict like it was yesterday. They were a canny enemy. We lost a lot of friends. Most of them pilots." Jones drifted off for a moment and cleared his throat. "Your kind are our most valuable commodity. We can always replace a technician or a mechanic, but those who have a natural edge behind the controls are something special. The commandant keeps me in the loop when it comes to new cadets. His praise for you in particular has been nothing short of glowing."

"Thank you, Admiral," Sutter said, continuing beyond the dorms and past the simulator buildings.

"I assume you've heard of the ongoing rebel elements popping up on Bolar and her surrounding systems?"

"It's one of the main subjects here on campus."

"Indeed. You'd think by now, decades after their planet fell, they'd understand the importance of being part of a strong empire." Jones sighed. "Unfortunately, they continue to be a thorn in our side. And because of their insolence, we've got no choice but to send in our best against them. That's why I'm here today, Cadet. I'd like you to come with me."

"Me?" Sutter thought about his high school sweetheart back home on Dylaria. It had been so long since he'd got to hold Kathy in his arms. "But, Admiral, I have a semester of my studies remaining."

The admiral stopped in the middle of the path. "Are you backing away from an opportunity to prove yourself in real combat?"

Sutter straightened his back again. "No, Admiral."

"I've looked over everything the commandant has given me on you. You remaining here for another six months would be a waste of talent." He pointed at the sky. "Up there is where you'll get a proper education."

Sutter unconsciously peered into the sky and then returned his attention to Jones. "It'd be an honor to join you, Admiral."

His new commander squeezed his shoulder with his large hand. "Good. Stick with me, *Lieutenant*, and I'll see to it you're always looked after."

"Logan!"

Logan opened his eyes to find Vernon's wrinkled face staring over him. He peered around the room, finding himself in his quarters aboard the *Corina II*.

"Are you okay?" he asked him.

Logan heaved himself up and threw the blankets aside. "Yeah, I was just adding some more of Sutter's memories to the collection."

Vernon grabbed Logan's boots near the door and passed them to him. "We're approaching the Hestan Star

System. Alira's getting cranky out there. We better not keep her waiting."

Logan got himself sorted and followed Vernon out of his quarters and into the cockpit, where Alira, as promised, was sitting at the controls.

She turned to the two men arriving behind her and relinquished her seat. "I've taken us out of hyperwarp. We're nearing the outer barrier of the Arcadian scope network."

Logan checked over the scopes, ensuring they were on track, and activated the flight plan he'd diligently put together the previous day. By his calculations, with the current solar activity taking place, they'd have the path to the detention facility they were after, but only if he was on his game. He flipped a series of switches, and all the cockpit's lights winked out, along with most of the ship's systems. "I hope no one here's afraid of the dark."

The *Corina II* entered the outer edge of the star system, and Logan pointed the vessel in the general direction of the small speck of light ahead. The trio didn't say a word. Not for hours. Even the goons Alira had brought with her kept it down to a dull roar when they poked their head in. After what seemed like an eternity later, along with several cups of coffee and the odd ration pack, they finally arrived.

"There it is." Logan slowed the craft and examined his scopes, keeping them on the right heading to ensure they didn't appear on the enemy's scopes.

Through the viewport, the enormous asteroid field took shape, filled with asteroids of every size imaginable. "Now comes the hard part." He piloted the vessel inside and plotted a course for the detention facility.

Alira took a seat next to Logan and stared across at him. She watched his fingers as they danced over the console. "Is it crazy to admit I somehow feel at ease with the Red Hawk at the controls?"

"Don't relax yet." Logan flew over the top of a sizeable asteroid and weaved closer to another, just to make her jump. He had to give her credit. She didn't flinch. Not even once.

But an alert sounding on her console did.

Vernon leaned over the back of her chair, and Logan checked the reading on his own screens. "Three Arcadian fighters."

Logan expected some security stationed at the facility. He had hoped it wasn't in the form of a fighter detachment. He steered the *Corina II* on an adjacent heading, past a vast grouping of asteroids, and double-checked to see if the ship was powered down to the levels they had been since entering the system.

"Could they have they've spotted us?" Alira asked.

"If they have, they're not making it obvious," Vernon told her. "If they loop around, we'll know we're in trouble."

Logan gave the man a knowing look and concentrated on his course, keeping a close eye on the fighters. Soon, the largest asteroid of the field, almost the size of a small planetoid, appeared. He slowed further and drifted toward it. He squinted to make a visual examination of it, and as he continued moving in, spotted a man-made structure on the northern-most tip of the giant space boulder. "There we go. There's our target."

Another alert rang out from the opposite console, and the trio examined the scopes, zooming in on a contained part of the base at the southern section.

"Crap!" Logan pulled up, and they moved away from the facility as quickly as he dared inside an asteroid field. He used the maneuvering thrusters to take them to a safe location behind another huge rock. He brought the ship to a full stop and locked down the helm.

Alira looked at the two men. "What the hell was that all about?"

"The base..." Logan sighed. "It's been fitted with a weapon platform."

ELEVEN

"Are you telling me there was no weapon platform the last time you were here?"

Vernon stood between the pair sitting in front of him, waiting for Logan to answer Alira's question.

"If there was I would have said so," Logan shot back at her. "They've obviously done some upgrades. Installing a weapon platform and stationing a squadron of fighters is a lot cheaper than replacing an entire system-wide scope network."

Briggs entered the cockpit, wedging himself through the door and pushing past Vernon. "This was a setup all along, wasn't it?"

Vernon lamented the grunt had likely been listening outside the cockpit. "This isn't the time—"

"Did it look like I was talking to you, old man?" He stepped closer to Alira. "I told you this was a bad idea."

Vernon could hardly blame the huge galoot for the mistrust between them. He'd grappled with it, too. He might not have considered the Bolarans his enemy any-more, but they obviously couldn't see past the bad blood.

"You really think we came all the way out here to hand you over to the Empire?" Logan said before the Bolaran woman had a chance to answer her soldier. "Frankly, you're not that important. And don't forget, it's you who wanted us to come here."

The cogs in Alira's head appeared to crank, and she nodded at Briggs. The man glared at Logan and left the cockpit, returning some much needed space to the tiny confines. "Okay, so what do we do now?" she asked

"The smartest thing would be to go back to Bolar." Logan checked his screens and prepared to find a course out of the asteroid field.

"I didn't come all this way to tuck my tail between my legs. We're here. Show me what the great Red Hawk can do."

Logan swiveled his chair toward Vernon. "What do you think?"

Vernon peered out at the huge asteroid they'd hidden behind. "I think it's time to dig for some of that Sutter ingenuity."

"Even if it means risking all our lives?"

"If we don't, we'll be risking everyone else's back in the Rim."

Logan tapped his controls, deep in thought. He rubbed his chin and glanced sideways at Alira. "The fighters..."

Alira raised her eyebrows. "The ones we passed in the asteroid field?"

"The only way we're getting into that base is making the Arcadians think we're one of them." Vernon nodded, having a fair idea where Logan was heading with his line of thought. "How do we do it?"

Alira put up a halting hand. "Hold on. How do we do what?"

"We're going to steal one of those fighters," Logan told her.

Alira stared back and forth between the two men. "Let me get this straight, we're somehow going to knock out one of these fighters, without the rest of the squadron knowing about it? Someone's then going to fly it into the facility and break Keller out? That's your plan?"

"Yes," Vernon and Logan replied in unison.

She brushed aside the length of hair getting into her eyeline. "Okay, say we seize a fighter, and say someone infiltrates the detention facility. How are they going to rescue Keller on their own? I brought six soldiers with me to storm that place. None of them will fit in that fighter."

"I won't be doing it by myself. Those fighters are T-class crafts," Logan said. "There's a compartment behind the pilot's seat. It'll be a tight squeeze, but someone else can come with me."

"How tight of a squeeze?" Alira asked.

"Probably too tight for any of your soldiers, or Vernon."

Alira pursed her lips together. "I should've guessed you guys were nuts."

Logan weaved the *Corina II* from asteroid to asteroid, as far away as possible from the Arcadian fighters, while making sure he could monitor them on the ship's scopes. From his days in the Fighter Corps, he knew how routine patrols operated. Rarely in an asteroid field would a squadron move together in a tight formation. If suddenly a wayward asteroid was more unpredictable than usual, having to implement a high-risk maneuver near other fighters could be catastrophic. And while the three Arcadians were well-spaced, they were still too close for Logan's liking. If he was going to seize one of the fighters, their compatriots would have to remain in the dark.

Several footsteps sounded behind him, and Vernon and Alira entered the cockpit. "The grapple's been loaded, and I've checked over the launch system," his mentor said. "Every ounce of power we can find has been routed to it. We shouldn't have a problem disabling the fighter. But you'll only get—"

"One shot. I know." Logan gestured to the seat next to him. "That's why you're going to be the one firing it."

Vernon sat warily, shifting into a slightly more comfortable position. He put his hands on the controls and activated the targeting computer. Logan, meanwhile, checked the scopes again, preparing for the right moment to pounce. Finally, a chance presented itself as one of the Arcadians swept off course, toward a heavily concentrated section of the asteroid field to continue its patrol.

"That's it. We've got one on their own." Logan took the ship from their safe haven and entered the field on an adjacent course with the ship's maneuvering thrusters. Several meteoroids pinged into their hull, but nothing big enough to cause any damage. With one eye on the scopes and the other on the viewport, he pressed on, doing his best to remain far enough away from the Arcadian fighter so as not to be picked up.

Alira grabbed the back of his chair, and her fingernails dug into the upholstery. Logan couldn't help but chuckle at her nervousness, considering the grandiose show she'd put on when they'd first met. He guessed everyone had their limits.

A wayward asteroid forced him to evade to starboard and another to port. He fought with the controls, doing everything he could to hold on with what limited maneuverability he had with such little power flowing through the bones of the small ship.

A larger asteroid appeared ahead of them.

"Perfect." Logan dived toward it. Tinier meteoroids bounced against the outer hull, along with a bigger one he didn't expect. The impact shuddered the cockpit and rattled them in their seats. "Sorry."

Logan parked the vessel behind the huge asteroid and examined the scopes. "The Arcadian fighter's coming about. Get ready with that grapple."

Lieutenant Moore yawned, weaving past the giant asteroid to port and plotting a course out of the heavily concentrated section of the field.

"My talents are being wasted here." He double-checked to ensure his comms were off and pointed the fighter at another asteroid, dodging it at the last second just to make sure he was still awake. "Half a year in this hellhole and what have I got to show for it?"

He sighed and prepared to fire the main thrusters to take him back to his colleagues so they could all return to the detention facility.

An alert wailed, and he craned his neck at the readings. A solitary contact appeared on his port stern. It was close. Really close.

"What the hell?"

Moore put one hand on the maneuvering lever and another on his comms, to send a message to the other pilots in his squadron. Something thudded against his hull, stopping him from making the attempt.

His screens went haywire, and all the lighting on his consoles winked out. Moore widened his eyes, now well and truly awake. He mashed down on all his keypads. But nothing responded.

Whatever had hold of him tugged him hard in the other direction. Through the viewport, another ship appeared. He couldn't tell the design from such close range, but it certainly wasn't a fighter.

They must have me in a grapple.

Another clunk sounded, and his momentum came to a halt. Moore tried again at the controls, only to be disappointed. A scratching noise emanated from below, and he peered beneath his legs. Whoever had him were trying to open the fighter's ventral hatch. He fumbled for his sidearm and grasped it tight in his hands.

The hatch blew, and he fell downward, ejecting from his craft onto a deck of some kind. A committee of six large men and a woman, all armed with rifles, welcomed him, pointing their weapons at his head. He held up his gun in his quaking hands only to have it smashed out of them.

The butt of a rifle launched at his face, and everything around him turned to darkness.

TWELVE

One by one, the more than twenty recruits brought aboard the *Defender* marched through the dark lower decks of the ORC destroyer. Novikova couldn't help but feel cramped. Even the *Ringwood* was more spacious. One thing was certain, though: the *Defender* was a ship of war.

"Nielsen, Penn, and Dravid!" the officer called toward the front of the line.

The three jokers from the carrier each raised their hands behind Novikova, and the officer ushered them forward. "These are your quarters," she told them.

Her offsider handed each of the men a data pad. "You've been assigned to the infantry contingent. Get settled in and report to your commanding officer at the top of the hour."

"Yes, sir," they all said unison, sliding the door to the tight confines of their new home. They squeezed inside, and the queue continued on.

The line thinned with the rest of the recruits assigned their accommodation and handed their assignments, until only Novikova remained. The officers led her around the corner and up to the next deck via the one of the *Defender's* elevators. They entered another corridor, and she stopped for a moment to take in the much nicer surroundings.

"Are you coming, recruit?" the most senior of the two asked.

"Uh, yeah." Novikova caught up to them, and they reached a door about halfway down.

"These are yours," the junior officer told her, opening it and revealing the inside of the quarters. It was twice the size of her little home aboard Telstar Station and had even more amenities. There was also only one bed, unlike the quarters every other recruit had been assigned.

"Are you sure this is mine?" Novikova asked.

The junior officer handed her a data pad.

Novikova shook her head. "Wait, this can't be right."

The two officers stared at her, unblinking, and seemingly fatigued, babysitting new recruits. "You're instructed to report to the *Defender's* executive officer," the senior of the pair informed her. "If you've got any problems, take it up with him."

With their job done, they disappeared down the other end of the corridor toward another elevator. Novikova glanced at her orders again and shrugged. She placed the data pad in her bag and entered her new home. The lights automatically illuminated, giving her an even better look.

For a moment, she smiled.

But it disappeared in a flash.

Her new quarters couldn't replace her childhood room. Nothing could.

***

Novikova took the elevator to the upper deck and stepped into the corridor. A large archway ahead of her led through to the bridge. She walked toward it and stopped at the threshold, taking in the buzz of activity. The casual atmosphere she was accustomed to on the *Ringwood* was nowhere to be seen. The men and women of the *Defender* were a well-drilled team, ranging from the very young to the very old.

"Recruit Novikova?"

She spun around to find a man standing behind her, with the rank pins of a commander on his uniform. "Commander Emovic?"

He nodded.

She straightened her back. "Jana Novikova reporting for duty, sir."

Emovic invited her inside his office. She followed him in, and he took a seat behind his desk. Novikova stood still in front of him. She wasn't used to all the formality yet but did her best, not wanting to make a poor impression. She caught a reflection of herself in the viewport, adorned in her new uniform. It was a little tight for her liking. Nothing like the casual attire she'd wear on Telstar Station in her free time.

"Take a seat, recruit," he told her. "How are you settling in?"

Novikova relaxed and sat in the solitary chair opposite him. "Fine, sir."

"Good. While the *Defender* might not be one of the prettiest vessels in the ORC fleet, she's got plenty of stories to tell. I'm sure you'll be a good addition with us."

"I'm not complaining, Commander. My quarters are more than I could've dreamed of." She pulled out the data pad with her orders on it and placed it on her lap. "However, there's something I'd like to discuss with you."

"Oh?"

"All the other recruits were crammed into quarters on the lower levels. Most were either assigned to infantry, tech division, or the engine room. My orders have me training in the flight and navigation section."

Emovic narrowed his eyes. "I fail to see what the problem is."

"Sir, I've only ever worked as an engineer. My time aboard the *Ringwood* was—"

"Recruit Novikova. The *Defender* has enough engineers. We also now have enough techs and infantrymen. What we're lacking are those who can take the helm."

"But, sir, I'm not a helmsman."

Emovic grabbed a data pad from the pile to his right and activated it. "Your testing would say otherwise. While you may have rarely conducted any of those duties on the *Ringwood*, the tests revealed a high aptitude required for flight control officers. It's been decided that your expertise would be better suited to this field to fill the void we have. While aboard the *Defender,* you'll train in helm operations. Eventually, you'll be granted status as a full flight officer with the rank of lieutenant. Depending on your progress and the further needs of the rebellion, you could even be assigned to fighter pilot training."

Novikova didn't know what to say. She'd never considered herself a pilot. Even during the times she'd taken the helm of the *Ringwood*, while she enjoyed it, she never thought she had the capability to do it full-time.

The commander finally cracked a smile. It was a small one. But it was there. "With that said, I'm sure our chief engineer could use someone to clean out the thruster exhausts. We can start you out as a third-class technician, if you'd like? It'd mean sharing quarters with three other crewmen."

"No, no," Novikova blurted out. "I've always been up for a challenge."

"Good. You have your training schedule on your pad. Report to your instructor tomorrow morning."

Novikova checked the pad and stood.

"You're dismissed, recruit," Emovic instructed her.

She turned and left the commander's office, allowing the door to close behind her. She leaned up against the bulkhead and thought back to the first time her father had let her take the family tractor for a ride. Unfortunately, few of those skills would assist her in her training. Ironically, it would be the tips and tricks taught to her by Kel Speer that would help her out the most.

THIRTEEN

"Are you ready back there?"

Logan opened the hatch of the small compartment behind the seat of his newly acquired fighter, finding Alira squeezed into the tiny space. She glared at him, constantly squirming to find a comfortable position. He tried not to smile, amused she was the one now locked up. "If you need anything, just knock."

He closed the hatch and sat in the pilot's seat, pressing out the wrinkles of the Arcadian flight suit they'd stripped from the fighter's previous owner. He put his helmet on and strapped it up. A green light flashed on his left-side console, and he pushed in the button next to it.

"Are you all buckled up, Logan?" Vernon asked over the comms.

Logan hooked the last of his belts over his shoulder and waist. "I am now."

"You better get out there. The other fighters are starting to head toward our position."

He put his hands on the maneuvering lever and powered up the main thrusters. "I'm on my way."

"Good luck out there."

Logan pulled Vernon's father's dog tags from his pocket, making sure he still had them. "I'll see you soon."

He switched off the comms and detached from the *Corina II*, moving slowly away from her to the other side of the asteroid. Ahead, the two fighters appeared, barreling in his direction.

"Captain Snell to Lieutenant Moore, do you read me?" the hail came over the comms.

Logan keyed in the special linguistic program they'd installed before departing. As far as Snell would know, whatever Logan said to him over the frequency would come across in Moore's voice. "I read you."

"What happened? You dropped off our scopes."

"Sorry, I thought I spotted something on this asteroid, so I took a detailed scan on the opposite side. Nothing turned up."

Silence lingered across the channel for a moment, and Logan wondered if the squadron leader believed him or not. He double-checked to make sure the linguistic program was operating properly.

"Fall in formation, Lieutenant," the captain finally said. *"We're returning to base."*

"Aye, sir." Logan moved toward the fighters as they turned. He followed them all the way to the detention facility, where the huge asteroid it had been constructed on filled his vision. The memories of when he'd first visited it as James Sutter came back to him all at once. He still couldn't remember the reason for visiting, but he definitely hadn't been piloting a fighter the last time around. It was an impressive structure, similar to Artemis, but on a much larger scale.

The flight deck door opened, and the squadron leader moved ahead of the other pair, pushing through and touching down inside the bay. Logan followed the other fighter and brought his craft down off to the side in one of the spare spaces allocated to the fighters. He powered down all his systems but kept his helmet on, waiting for the landing bay doors to close. Once they did, the section saturated with breathable air, and the two other pilots lifted their canopies. Logan remained in wait, keeping an eye on them walking across to the internal door.

One of them stopped and took off his helmet.

"Just keep going," Logan muttered. If they were going by strict regulations, they'd proceed to the briefing room to go over their notes and data logs. Unfortunately, being away from the core worlds, few pilots ever followed the guidelines. He decided to open his canopy and waved at him. He could only hope Snell would take it as a sign that Logan would catch up to them.

Snell and the other pilot looked at each other for a moment and then back at Logan.

Keep moving...

They finally shrugged and stepped into the outer corridor.

Logan unbuckled his harness and launched himself out of the cockpit, sliding across the wing and jumping onto the deck. He rushed over to the lockers on the far wall and opened one up, revealing a large uniform inside. He moved on to the next, finding another only one size down. The other three were all similar. The final locker contained the smallest he could find. "This'll have to do."

He yanked it from the coat hanger, found another helmet, and ran back to the fighter, grabbing a ladder and slamming it against the hull. He climbed up it and opened the hatch behind his seat. Alira stared up at him, shielding her eyes from the light. "How was the trip?" he asked her.

She didn't answer him and stumbled out of the compartment, stretching out her arms and legs.

Logan handed her the uniform. "I hope this doesn't look too ridiculous on you."

Alira yanked the clothes from him and went down the ladder onto the deck. She started to undress from her civvies, not embarrassed in the least.

Logan joined her and checked the door, waiting for the deck crew to arrive. They couldn't be too far off. "You're going to need to hurry."

Alira threw her shirt at him, and he instinctively turned, catching a glimpse of her. She was as athletic as he imagined, but there were also plenty of war wounds. Several scars were etched around her back and sides, and some nasty burn marks dotted her legs. She quickly finished putting on the Arcadian uniform and put her hands on her hips. As expected, it was too big for her petite frame. Logan could only hope no one noticed.

He handed her the spare helmet. "Here, put this on."

She placed it on her head, and the door opened. The deck crew piled out in their grimy overalls with tool kits in their hands.

"Now, do as I do." Logan set off with Alira close in tow.

They marched through the middle of the group, and the mechanics parted as they went. None of them even blinked an eyeball at them as they made it all the way into the outer corridor. He breathed a sigh of relief, and the door closed behind them.

Alira removed her helmet. "Where to now?"

"You're going to need a computer." He tried to recall the layout of the facility which was scattered inside the mind of James Sutter. He peered down one end of the corridor and then pointed at the other. "Down there."

They headed off and rounded the corner, passing uniformed Arcadians and other staff along the way. Logan took off his helmet, forgetting he still had it on, and they continued into a small junction room off to the side, near an elevator. He opened the door, revealing the tight confines of the space. Alira stepped inside, and Logan stood in front of her while she hooked up the computer hacking device she'd brought with her.

The screen in the junction came to life, and a plethora of code and other data he couldn't make head or tails of flashed before them. Her fingers moved just as quickly across the keypad. "This isn't the first time you've done this kind of stuff, is it?"

"Not exactly." Her eyes didn't waver from the screen. A map appeared on it, revealing the entire facility. "Does this look familiar to you?"

Logan checked to see if the coast was clear and turned back to examine it. He pointed at their position and ran his finger down the elevator shaft. "This'll definitely lead us to the detention section. But to get in there—"

"Leave that to me." She pulled out the device and pocketed it, taking out another gadget.

He led her to the elevator, and she waved it over the panel beside the door. It remained red for a moment, then blinked green. The entry opened, and she entered.

"Well, are you coming with me or not?"

Logan warily followed, and the door shut. Alira set the car in motion, and they fired down into the heart of the asteroid. A strange sense of claustrophobia came over him, but before he could delve too much into it, the elevator opened, revealing another long corridor.

They passed by some guards and a large sign overhead informing them they were entering the detention section. At the end of the corridor, they stopped at the only way in or out. Alira tilted her head at Logan, and he looked at her knowingly. On either side of them, guards were almost breathing down their necks. The Bolaran woman sneakily pulled out her device and held it in her palm, waving it over the panel beside the door.

They waited.

And waited.

It didn't turn green.

Alira furrowed her brow and tried again.

It remained red.

"What's going on here!" the guard behind her asked.

Logan swore he could feel the pit of his stomach churn and the gun of the guard behind him rise.

FOURTEEN

Logan balled his right hand into a fist, ensuring the guards around him didn't notice. Taking on two men was one thing. Taking them on while they were pointing rifles in their backs was quite another.

Alira remained calm, again trying to achieve access via the panel beside the door. "I'm not sure what's going on," she said in answer to the guard peering over her shoulder. She slipped the device into the cuff of her shirt and held up her wrist. "I had my authorization chip updated yesterday."

The guard glanced at his colleague behind Logan.

"Let me try one last time." Alira put her hand up against the panel, no doubt slipping the device in her palm, away from the sight of the Arcadians.

Logan held his breath, determining what his first move would be against the two guards. The panel remained red as it went through the process of identifying Alira. Logan put all his weight on his left heel and prepared to swivel to rush the guard behind him. Every move he'd have to make played out in his head along with how the pair of Arcadians would counter him.

Still red.

Logan hoped Alira was preparing herself, too.

Still red.

He gazed up at the three cameras pointing at their position, wondering how many more guards would be waiting for them once their cover was blown.

Still red.

He eyed the guard opposite him. The suspicion in his features continued to exacerbate.

Still red.

The end of the guard's gun touched Logan's back.

Still red.

"There we go!"

Logan's mouth dropped agape at the panel glowing a miraculous green. The door clicked and swooshed open.

Alira put her hand in her pocket, and the guards shuffled backward into their initial position, dropping their guns by their sides.

"Make sure you get your authorization checked," the most senior of the pair warned Alira. "A lot of the guys down here a pretty trigger happy."

She thanked him for his advice and moved through the door, ushering Logan along. The door slid shut behind them, and they strolled casually down the inner corridor.

"What the hell was all that about?" Logan whispered to her.

"Just be thankful I got us in here at all," she said. "The tech devised to do this kind of thing—"

"Thankful!" he snapped a little too loudly, passing by another guard. "I'm not the one who wants to be here."

"You are if you want an alliance." Alira led him around the next corner, and they approached the prisoner area. They went through the next access point, and she looked at the numbers above all the doors, counting them under her breath until they reached the cell she was after.

Alira darted her eyes left and right to ensure the coast was clear, waiting for some guards to disappear at the end of the corridor. She placed her device over the panel, and it blinked green. The door clicked exactly like the one at the entrance and slid open.

Alira put her foot over the threshold and poked her head inside the dark confines. "Michael?"

No one answered, but a shuffling noise permeated in the void. She took another step, and Logan shadowed her into the center of the cell. The lights blinked on and bathed the entire room in a horrible brightness. Both Logan and Alira shielded their eyes and turned to a figure standing at the door next to the switch.

Logan let the spots filter from his sight and allowed them to adjust to the illumination. In that time, Alira dove toward the figure, and the two wrapped their arms around each other. They locked lips, sharing a passionate embrace. Logan quickly deduced their mission was a little more personal than just rescuing the leader of Bolar's rebellion.

Alira and the incarcerated man eventually unclasped themselves from each other. "This is James Sutter... I mean Nathan Logan," she said. "And Logan, this is Michael Keller."

Logan went over to the couple, immediately noticing the pale-blue eyes of the man. His skin was strangely unnatural, too, with an unhealthy chalkiness to it.

"Never in my wildest dreams would I have ever guessed I'd be rescued by the Red Hawk," Keller quipped.

Alira motioned to the door. "Come on, let's get out of here."

The trio didn't dally and rushed out of the cell, taking it easy at every corner to make sure they wouldn't be spotted. They finally reached the exit, but it was too late. Alira put her device over the panel, and a klaxon blared around them.

"They're onto us." Alira waved the device, but the door wouldn't open.

"A problem like earlier?" Logan asked, checking behind him for any Arcadians.

"If they know you're here to take me, they've figured out by now their system was compromised. We'll have to do this another way." Keller turned to Alira. "I assume you brought it with you?"

His wife, partner, or who knows what, took a cable from the cuff of her shirt. Keller spun around and opened a patch of skin on the back of his neck, revealing a port for the cable built into bone, not unlike something found on a computer. Alira plugged the cable into the port and yanked the cover from the panel on the wall, inserting the other end inside.

"What the hell is this?" Logan blurted out.

Vernon hadn't moved. Not for hours. Which was impressive, considering how weary his bones and muscles got sitting still for such a long period. He'd surely pay for it later. But right now, he didn't care.

He thought at that point he'd have seen some sign from the detention facility to inform him Logan was alive. Though no sign might have been all the answer he needed. He dropped his head solemnly, and loud footfalls sounded behind him. He didn't need to turn to know who it was. The man's body odor was unmistakable.

Briggs placed a hand on the headrest of the copilot's seat and stared out at the asteroid where the *Corina II* remained near as cover. "You know as well as I, old man, that they're both dead."

"I didn't realize Bolarans gave up so easily," Vernon snapped, surprising himself at how bitter the words came out.

A demonic grin curled on Briggs' weathered face. "I'm a realist. This was a fool's errand from the beginning. Keller was already lost to us."

"So, what do you want to do now? Run back home? The Bolarans I fought in my day were a lot tougher than you."

Briggs' smile faded. "Your pretty mouthy for a sack of bones. You realize I could crush your skull with my fist, right?"

"Then who would you get to pilot this thing out of the asteroid field?"

The grunt didn't seem to have an answer. Suddenly, an alert sounded on the scopes, bringing an end to the steely confrontation. Vernon checked his screen, and a bogey appeared on the edge of their range. "Well, I'll be damned. A transport ship. It's got to be them."

Briggs leaned in to get a look for himself. "If it is, they're not alone."

Vernon nodded as the second bogey materialized from the detention facility. It had the same transponder code as one of the fighter's they'd come across earlier. "We'll have to give them a hand. Take the copilot's position. I need someone at combat."

The Bolaran soldier wedged himself in at the seat next to him and activated the targeting computer. While Vernon wasn't out of practice piloting a ship, the vessel wasn't the original *Corina*, and traversing an asteroid field was difficult even when he'd been in his prime.

He directed them away from their cover and powered

up all the remaining systems. The controls were sluggish. Much more than he expected.

Definitely not the Corina...

Ahead, the small transport craft appeared, and the comms panel blinked. Without needing to be asked, Briggs activated the channel.

"We're coming home, Vernon," Logan said through the cockpit's speakers. *"And we're bringing company."*

"We see them," Vernon responded. "Make sure you give me a good shot at them."

"We'll try. Don't miss."

Vernon directed the *Corina II* around a cluster of small asteroids and powered toward a slightly larger one, stopping just behind it. He checked his scopes, readying for Logan's craft and the fighter to pass. As hoped, they both charged by the asteroid, as quickly as he expected. Vernon pounced, moving out and going in pursuit.

Briggs set the crosshairs on the Arcadian fighter, and Vernon continued ducking around the many asteroids in their path. For a moment, he felt like a young pilot who thought he could take on the whole universe.

The targeting computer flashed red, and Briggs fired.

The Arcadian pilot attempted to evade the missile, but he was too late. His craft exploded, forcing Vernon to avoid the debris.

"Nice shooting," he told Briggs.

The soldier merely grunted, got up from his seat, and walked out of the cockpit.

Vernon activated the comms and plotted a course to rendezvous with the transport. "Time to come home, Logan."

FIFTEEN

Logan hadn't taken his eyes from the man since arriving back on the ship. His hypnotic stare was one thing, but it was the paleness of his skin, his slightly shaky hands, and the sparsely covered head of hair which confounded him the most. Logan knew as well as anyone how the Empire's interrogation techniques could be barbaric, but he'd never seen a prisoner like Keller.

Logan and Vernon stood in the tiny sickbay watching on as one of the Bolaran soldiers, who acted as a medic, too, examined Keller.

"How is he?" Alira asked, standing by her leader's side.

"He's alive." The soldier checked over his medical probe and placed it in his pocket. "However, with every-thing the Arcadians have done to him, he probably shouldn't be."

"I'll take that as a compliment," Keller said.

Alira looked deep into the sickly man's eyes and turned to the medic. "How much of this has to do with the, uh, enhancements?"

"A lot, I would guess," came the reply. "But for the moment, he's not going to die."

"That sounds like a clean bill of health to me." Keller gestured to the exit. "That'll be all."

The medic nodded and left the sickbay, closing the door behind him. Keller swung his legs over the side of the bed and hopped down, wincing in pain.

"I never thought I'd do this, but I suppose I should thank you both for coming to get me," he said to Logan and Vernon. "Two heroes of the Empire. I don't think anyone will believe it when they find out that Bolarans and Arcadians worked together."

Logan glared at him. "We're not Arcadians."

"If we were, you'd likely be dead," Vernon added.

"My apologies." Keller put his hands up in surrender and narrowed his eyes. "I suppose I have to ask. Why did you come after me?"

"They came seeking an alliance," Alira told him, before the two men had a chance to answer.

Keller laughed from the pit of his stomach. "And you promised them an alliance if they helped rescue me?"

"There was no other way to get you out."

"I would've figured it out."

"No, you wouldn't have."

"I—"

"Stop this!" Vernon demanded. "I didn't come here to listen to you bicker. You owe us an explanation for everything that's happened here. Why did you travel to the core worlds? How did the Arcadians capture you? And what the hell is that thing in the back of your neck?"

"Are we safely away from the detention facility?" Keller asked Logan.

"There's no one on our tail," he said. "We're safe for the time being."

"Good. Yes, I suppose I've got a bit of explaining to

do." The rebellion leader rubbed his jittery hands together and sat back on the edge of the bed. "With our cause on shaky ground, I decided to go to the core worlds on an important mission."

Vernon leaned up against the bulkhead. "What kind of mission?"

"I wanted information."

Logan and Vernon raised their eyebrows at each other.

"I left Bolar and took a small team to Deltex V, intending to infiltrate a facility there and download all the data I could get my hands on," Keller continued.

"What kind of facility?" Vernon asked.

"It's home to a vast computer database." Logan recalled doing war game exercises near it when it was being constructed but never visited when it went fully operational.

"Effectively, it's an information hub for all the comings and goings inside Arcadian territory," Keller told them. "There's likely more knowledge there than anywhere else in the entire Empire."

"Quite an impressive feat getting in there, considering how secure it is. How did you do it?"

The Bolaran smiled and revealed the port in the back of his neck. "Artemis Unit isn't the only place where the galaxy's best and brightest are conducting experiments. As you know, any fight against the Arcadians requires guile. No one can take the challenge to them directly and expect to win. We have to be creative. Our best scientists have been working for years, under the cloak of darkness, away from the prying eye of the Empire, to come up with all kinds of ways to bring them down. What you're looking at is one of them."

Logan moved closer to the bed. "Are you...human?"

"Oh, I'm human." Keller chuckled. "But part of me has been replaced with some of the most advanced technology ever developed on Bolar. Even with all the technological marvels humanity has achieved, the human brain is still one of the greatest designs conceived. It's processing power on so many levels just can't be replicated."

Logan recalled the device Alira had brought with her on the mission to rescue her leader. "So, what are you saying? You're like a human code breaker."

"It's more complicated than that," the Bolaran woman interrupted. "Not only does the technology incorporated inside Keller give him the ability to integrate into any system and access it, but it also allows him to store data at levels we simply can't do with the hardware available."

Keller pulled up his shirt, revealing lumps on each side of his spine. "My mission was to download the entire database of Deltex V."

Logan shook his head, almost unbelieving at what was sitting before him. He wanted to tell the man he was kook. But he'd witnessed firsthand what was possible at Artemis. What the Bolarans had done was remarkable, even if it was a little crude. "What happened on the mission?"

Keller paused for a moment and glanced at Alira. "Everything was going smoothly. We managed to get through the outer security perimeter without a problem. We then infiltrated the inside of the facility, coming up against no resistance. I hooked myself up to the main data hub and began the download."

"So, how did you get found out?" Vernon asked.

"Strangely enough, it was an Arcadian soldier. Of course, we were disguised as computer technicians, but one of my men decided to wear scuffed boots on the mission. The soldier picked up on it. Naturally, no employee of the Empire would ever show up to work without a shined pair of boots. It was a small mistake. And we paid for it." Keller stopped and shrugged off some pain. "All my men were lost—"

"But you survived?"

"I think they knew what I was doing. They wanted me alive so that they could study me."

"And they brought you to Hestan?"

Keller nodded. "They did everything but slice me up. I have a feeling that was their next course of action since no amount of torture, Kowalski Machine sessions, or trimurilene injections, got them what they needed. They'd never seen anything like me and needed to know how I broke all their security encryptions while downloading a substantial part of their database."

"Let me get this straight," Logan said, perplexed. "You're telling me you were injected with trimurilene and you still didn't spill any secrets."

A glint appeared in Keller's eyes. "That's right. It didn't turn me into a vegetable either."

"How's that possible?"

"With a little help." The Bolaran tapped the port on the back of the neck. "There's only one antidote to trimurilene, and that's cortaveron. But it must be administered instantly. I devised a way to store the cortaveron in my body and use my processor to regulate the dispersal in a safe matter should I be captured. Like most of what you see before you, I wasn't sure it would work. But here we are."

Vernon crossed his arms, examining Keller as if he were a bug under a microscope. "So, that's the reason you look like death warmed up then?"

"Ironically, no." A thin grin appeared on Keller's

morbid face but quickly faded. "It's the components inside me doing this. Humans aren't meant to do this to themselves, and because of it, I've shortened my life considerably. But I'm hoping it was all worth it if I was able to download what I went to Deltex V for."

"Which was what exactly?"

Keller's smile returned. "We've been thinking about our struggle with the Empire the wrong way for a long time now. When we go up against the Arcadians, we see them as a megalithic bloc—an unwavering army of darkness with an impenetrable shield protecting them. We should look at them as if they were a snake."

"You want to chop off the head..." Vernon seemed to be lost in another place for a moment. "The emperor?"

Keller nodded. "He's been in seclusion for many years. But ultimately, he's the puppet master who's presided over all of this. The last time he appeared in public was decades ago. Its widely known he doesn't reside in his palace on Arcadia anymore, so that's why I came here. To find out where he is so we can cut the snake's head off once and for all."

"You think no one's ever thought of that?" Vernon scoffed. "The man's had more attempts on his life than I can count on both hands. Probably more. That, and his age, was one of the reasons he went into solitude. Assassinating him is a fantasy."

Logan was getting weary of the conversation. Especially so after hearing of the Bolaran's pipedream to assassinate the only person in the galaxy it was impossible to kill. "Are we going to get an alliance or not?"

"An alliance?" Keller coughed and scratched the back of his neck. "I don't think that would do you much good."

Logan balled his hand into a fist. "And why's that?"

"Haven't you heard?" He gazed at both Logan and Vernon. "Gelbrana's been completely destroyed. The Empire are on the march through the Rim."

Logan's heart sank.

Jana...

SIXTEEN

"There's far more thruster controls to navigate on the *Defender* than there were on the *Ringwood*."

Novikova ran her hands over the workstation, taking in the entirety of the destroyer's helm settings. Her trainer, Lieutenant Reimer, walked to the other side of the console and grinned.

"It comes in handy when you want to get out of the way of incoming fire," he said. "Ore transports don't get into as much trouble as we do."

"You'd be surprised." She checked over the toggles to her left. "It doesn't help that on the *Ringwood* the navigational switches were on the other side."

"Just think of it like this; everything starts from the left, like a book." He pointed at the helm. "Set your course here, plug in your speed there, and control your manual thrusters over here."

"As easy as that, huh?" Novikova chuckled, seeing humor in the fact that the man teaching her was at least ten years younger than her. And she wasn't that old. She imagined Reimer had dabbled with flying on his home colony and, when the war broke out, he'd rallied to the call. She hoped she was as good a student as he was a teacher. As it stood, the Empire was continuing to cut a swathe through the Outer Rim, and there wouldn't be much left if something didn't turn in their favor soon.

"Are you ready to do some maneuvers?" Reimer asked.

"Uh, sure. Should I—"

"Plot a course directly ahead. I want you to use manual thrusters only." He put his hands behind his back and stepped to the other side of her. "Once you've got a straight line down pat, we'll see how you go at turning."

Novikova hovered her fingers over the helm and locked in a course, preparing to fire the thrusters. Then an alert sounded at the rear of the bridge. She stopped, hoping she'd done nothing wrong.

Captain Pollock, loitering around the combat station, moved toward communications. "What is it?"

The fresh-faced woman, even younger than Reimer, swiveled slightly in her chair. "We're receiving an automated distress call."

"From where?"

"The Metra Star System."

"The scope outpost?"

She nodded. "From last report there was a corvette stationed there on patrol."

Pollock walked to the front of the bridge. "How far away are we?" he asked Reimer.

"We can be there in under two hours," Novikova's instructor told him.

"Plot a course and get us underway. Probably best you take the reins."

"Yes, sir." Reimer put a comforting hand on Novikova's shoulder, and she quickly relinquished the seat, letting the more experienced officer resume his regular duties.

It didn't take him long to move the *Defender* into hyperwarp. It also didn't take long for the casual atmosphere around the bridge to disappear. Reimer instructed Novikova to remain by his side, making sure she watched everything he did. Eventually, the *Defender* approached their destination and entered sub-light at the edge of the system.

Pollock stopped by Ensign Georgiou at the scopes. "What are you picking up out here?"

"We'll have to move closer, sir," he informed his superior. "The outpost's near the sixth planet. At this range from the disturbance of the gas giant, my readings are hazy at best."

"Leaving us to potentially walk into an Arcadian ambush." Pollock sighed. "Reimer, take the ship in, nice and easy. Combat, keep your finger on the trigger."

"Aye, sir," came the replies.

The *Defender* continued on, pushing toward the sixth planet. The huge purple orb appeared as if a jewel in the night, lit up by the dazzling yellow star at the heart of the system. It was a lovely sight, like so much in space, but Novikova had learned how many dangers the infinite abyss concealed with its magnificence. She closed her eyes, and her parents entered her mind, along with all the others who'd fallen. Images flashed of her father's cheeky grin, her mother's flowing dark hair, and her husband's broad shoulders and strong chest. Then Logan emerged through a foggy haze. She wondered if he was lost to her as well.

"Approaching orbit."

Novikova snapped her eyes open to Lieutenant Reimer informing the captain of the *Defender's* position. Behind her, Pollock prowled like a lion. A slightly jittery one at that.

"Continue on to the outpost," he ordered.

Reimer pressed in the commands, bringing the ship parallel to the gas giant and maneuvering across the planet.

Pollock went over to his communications officer. "Are we picking up any traffic over the comms?"

She shook her head. "Nothing."

"Which can mean only two things. Either the Arcadians are gone or they're concealing themselves."

Silence lingered throughout the bridge until something emerged on the backdrop of the planet. Novikova shifted toward the viewport while audible gasps went up around her. Pollock joined her to take in the sight of the fragments dancing about.

"Scopes!" he bellowed. "What's the composition of that debris field?"

There wasn't a response at first, so Pollock and Novikova turned to find the glum face of Georgiou staring at his screens. "I'd estimate were looking at the debris of the outpost and the ORC corvette," he said. "Give or take a few thousand tons, adjusting for the likely event some of it burned up in the planet's atmosphere."

More death...

"Any survivors?" Pollock asked.

Georgiou shook his head. "There's not much left out there that could be refuge to anyone."

"Wait, Captain!"

Every eye on the *Defender's* bridge gazed across to the communications officer. "I'm picking up something over the comms."

Pollock hurried over to her. "What is it?"

"It's faint, but it's there." She put the audio over the speakers, and a harsh pinging noise filtered through.

"That's Arcadian code," Novikova muttered.

Pollock grasped the back of the communication officer's chair. "Where's that emanating from? Are they inside the atmosphere?"

She double-checked all her readings. "No, it's coming from the debris field. I'm sending the coordinates to the scopes now."

Pollock marched over to Georgiou, and he acknowledged he'd received the coordinates. "Well?"

"We'll have to move in closer," he told the captain. "There's too much interference."

"Reimer—"

"On it, sir," the lieutenant replied.

Novikova returned to the helmsman's side, and he edged the *Defender* ever nearer, weaving through some of the debris and coming to a halt.

"There we are," Georgiou confirmed. "Looks like the signal's originating from an EV suit."

"An Arcadian pilot?" Pollock pondered.

"Quite possibly, sir."

"With the time that's passed, they could very well be alive, too." He scratched his chin. "Reimer, take some infantry and go and get them."

SEVENTEEN

Keller sat in a chair at the table of the rear compartment while everyone, including the Bolaran soldiers, meandered around the room like a bad smell. They were just as curious as Logan was at what was about to happen. Though he'd probably have been more fascinated if it wasn't the lingering concern about the news Novikova's home had been wiped from existence. He could only hope she was safe aboard the *Ringwood*. Or at the very least, as far away from Gelbrana as possible.

Across from him, Vernon remained quiet, his focus wavering between Keller and the ceiling. Logan wondered if he was thinking of the innocent Gelbranans who'd been so mercilessly massacred, or maybe about the ramifications of it for the rest of the Outer Rim.

Alira took a cable and plugged it into the computer on the far bulkhead. She unwound it and traipsed over to Keller. He exposed the port in the back of his neck, and she made the connection. Keller immediately winced. Logan contemplated if the discomfort was caused by linking with the ship's data core, or the pain he'd surely been living with since becoming the ungodly creation sitting before him. He often thought how hard done by he was, considering what he'd gone through at Artemis, but at least he hadn't been transformed into a human-cybernetic freakshow.

"Are you ready?" Alira asked him.

He nodded, and she went back to the computer, tapping her fingers on the keypad. Keller grimaced again, and the screen lit up with a series of code, much too complicated for Logan to understand. A holographic projection appeared above the table, and files materialized.

"Can you access them?" Logan asked.

"Why don't you do the honors?" Keller invited him.

Logan glanced at Alira, who nodded at him, and then across at Vernon, who'd barely moved since entering the room. Logan placed his hands in the hologram, shifting around the projections and opening random files. A series of star charts appeared, and he stepped back to take in their enormity.

"Fleet movements." Alira joined them at the table. "From all across the Empire."

"At least to the point this was downloaded," Keller chimed in.

Logan moved on to the next file, revealing communications logs. "Reports sent via the facility to be filed by admin on Arcadia."

"All worth examining to see if we can find patterns to their tactics."

Logan exited the file and found another. Inside it was nothing but a blank projection with R and D in bold text at the top. One of the soldiers, Briggs, rounded the table.

"Research and Development?" he said. "Can they be accessed?"

"They're heavily encrypted," Keller replied. "Even I'm struggling to crack them."

"Don't strain yourself." Alira squeezed his shoulder. "We'll try again later."

As if taking that as a cue, Logan continued working through the rest of the data.

Alira put up a hand. "Go back. What's that? Fleetwide communication codes?"

"Which would now be obsolete, since the Arcadians are aware I downloaded all of this," Keller said wearily. "Keep going."

After a while, sifting through it became quite laborious, but regardless of what the Bolaran leader might have claimed, they were sitting on a treasure trove of information. The ORC leadership would be well impressed. That's if Keller let them take the find back with them to the Rim.

"None of what we've seen here will win a war against the Empire." Keller grimaced and grabbed at his neck. "There's only one thing that might give us that chance."

The projection went a little haywire, and Keller's thoughts took control of proceedings, flicking through the files with his mind as if they were old-fashioned pieces of paper. "We've known for a long time the emperor hasn't been on Arcadia and that his whereabouts have been a closely guarded secret. We've had no idea where to look. However, now, we should be able to take an educated guess."

Dozens of lines of text appeared, and Logan squinted at the data hovering above the table. "Holo comms logs?"

Keller nodded. "All have been transmitted within the last year at regular intervals. And all directed to the emperor's council building on Arcadia."

The realization of what Logan was looking at hit him all at once. "The emperor's conversing with his council via this holo channel."

"Where does it emanate from?" Alira asked.

The holographic files disappeared, and a star chart replaced it. Keller zoomed in with his mind to a system containing five planets, pushing further onward to the third, and then to its solitary moon. "All roads lead to the moon of Magnus III."

Logan tried to remember if Sutter had ever visited but came up short. He likely hadn't, considering there was nothing within fifteen light-years of the Magnus Star System. "It's located on the other side of the Empire. You'd have to go through the core worlds to get there. You can count on there been plenty of roadblocks along the way."

"This was never going to be easy."

Logan stared across at Vernon, who remained his typical statuesque self. "You haven't uttered a word. What do you think?"

The man didn't so much as flinch at being called out. "Keller's right. We can't beat the Arcadians. And no matter what we do, the Rim may already be lost. Perhaps we can at least fracture the Empire."

Everyone in the room turned to him, and he continued.

"It's always been said the Empire, while large, isn't necessarily harmonious. The members of the council share one thing—their differences. If the emperor's out of the equation—"

"There might be civil war." Logan rubbed his chin and paced toward Alira. He spun back around. "Occupations of Bolar, Thandeena, and the Outer Rim would be quite difficult if that were the case."

"It won't be easy achieving a feat of such magnitude." Vernon eyed the Bolaran leader. "To get close to the emperor, you'll need all the help you can get."

"Is that an offer?" Keller asked.

Vernon put out his hand. "There's no reason we can't continue to help each other."

Keller tapped his fingers on the table and pulled the cable from his neck. The hologram disappeared, and he shook Vernon's hand. "To the emperor's glorious death."

EIGHTEEN

Plot the course there. Lock in the speed here. And control the thrusters over there.

Novikova stared at the helm while the *Defender* raced away from the Metra Star System at hyperwarp. She hadn't stopped studying since arriving on the ship and was enjoying the practical lessons, even if they were a little daunting. While Lieutenant Reimer seemed to have the utmost confidence in her, she wondered if perhaps she was in over her head. Ever since the rebellion against the Empire broke out, she'd struggled to forgive herself for not answering the call. She closed her eyes and tried to push away the image of her parents' corpses from her mind.

It was all for nothing.

Novikova reopened her eyes and lost herself in the swirl of the stars through the viewport. The *Defender* hadn't remained at Metra for long. Captain Pollock didn't want to risk being caught in another ambush, so he got them back on the move as quickly as possible. She scrunched up her face and rubbed her temples, attempting to concentrate. She pondered visiting Commander Emovic's office again and requesting reassignment to the engine room. At least down there she could disappear in her work.

Stop trying to hide.

A hand touched her shoulder, and she jolted to life.

Lieutenant Reimer quickly pulled his hand from her, noticing the discomfort. "Sorry, Novikova. I didn't mean to startle you."

"I, uh." She frowned. "It's okay. I was just..."

He smiled at her. There was an understanding in the kid's features. He reminded her of Jeddy Grayson from the *Ringwood*. Only more confident. And more intelligent. "Don't worry, I was just going to ask you for a report."

It was one of the first procedures she'd been taught. For a moment she had to think about it, before finally checking the central monitor on her console. "Uh, we're continuing on course for the Brilkian Star System at eight-point-three times the speed of light."

"Have you had to make any adjustments?"

Novikova nodded. "I had to alter for a disturbance from the Kerton Cluster pulsar. There were also reports of meteors on the edge of the Trevani Star System forcing me to plot us around the sector adjacent. We'll only lose two-point-one hours from our initial projection."

"Good. It doesn't seem like you've got any problems with hyperwarp maneuvers."

She was about to say something when Captain Pollock walked onto the bridge and made a beeline for the pair. "Recruit Novikova, come with me, please."

Her heart skipped a beat, and she immediately stood. Reimer took her seat at the helm, and she hurried after Pollock, who quickly departed the bridge. He led her to an elevator and directed the car to deck three.

Would he think I'm speaking out of turn if I broke the ice?

She'd never been so meek aboard the *Ringwood.* Never once had she ever wavered from telling Captain Estrada what she thought. Luckily for her, Pollock took the initiative first.

"How's your training proceeding?" he asked.

"Good, sir," she said. "Lieutenant Reimer's an excellent instructor."

He nodded, and more silence ensued. At that moment, she considered asking him for the transfer. The doors swooshing open stopped her, and Pollock motioned her down the corridor where they turned into a tiny room. The tight confines were dark, but the large screen on the bulkhead, looking out into another brightly lit space, produced enough light to give her a fair idea where she was. On the other side of the screen, a woman in a medical gown sat at a table.

"Don't worry, she can't see us inside the brig," Pollock assured her, closing the door behind them.

"Is that the Arcadian pilot?" she asked.

He nodded. "Her injuries were minor. When we brought her in for questioning, let's just say she wasn't overly cooperative. No amount of time on the Kowalksi Machine helped, so we injected her with trimurilene."

Novikova's stomach clenched. She remembered her experience with Kel Speer aboard Telstar Station all too well when he'd beaten her to a pulp, wanting answers to the ORC leadership's location. His final act was to threaten her with the truth-telling serum, which would have left her in a vegetative state. The hollow eyes of the pilot revealed she was near to that exact point. "What am I doing here, Captain?"

"I want you to listen to something." Pollock pressed a

button on the panel in front of him and leaned in. "Please tell us your name."

The Arcadian jerked, but her eyes remained deathly still. They bored through the screen as if she could see them.

Her mouth finally moved.

"My name is... James Sutter."

Vernon stepped over the threshold into the *Corina II*'s cockpit to find Logan sitting on the arm of the pilot's seat. The younger man peered out at the stars as if he were lost somewhere amongst them.

"What's going on inside that melon of yours?" he said to him.

A slight chortle escaped Logan's mouth, likely because it hadn't been the first time he'd been asked the question.

Vernon took a seat next to him at the copilot's position to soothe his weary bones. "You haven't said anything since we left Keller's little presentation."

Logan checked their auto-nav course. "What would you like me to say? You and I both know trying to assassinate the emperor is crazy."

"No one knows that more than me."

"But?"

"But it could be the only course of action we have left."

"I can't believe what I'm hearing."

"In what sense?"

"The fact that you're entertaining this." Logan shook his head. "When we first met, you were all about playing it safe. Or at least thinking out a scenario before making a rash decision. I was the risk-taker, remember?"

Vernon steepled his fingers together and became adrift in the past. So much from his days as a pilot for the Empire came flooding back to him. None more so than the memory of watching Corina die. "Desperate times..."

Silence lingered between the pair.

"Do you trust them?" Logan asked.

"Hmm?"

"The Bolarans?"

"Not at all." Vernon snapped out of the past. "They likely don't trust us either. But at least we share a common foe."

"You really believe if we can somehow take out the emperor, we could topple the Empire?"

"Topple it? No. Split it? Maybe." Vernon coughed. "Keller was right. From the outside, the Empire appears impenetrable, but it's built on a house of cards. All it'd take would be someone to cause a disruption. I don't know whether his death could bring about a civil war, but it may give us the chance we need to regroup. Time for the Outer Rim, the Bolarans, and the Thandeeans to band together to give the Arcadians something to contend with."

"You still speak of an alliance," Logan said, not too convinced. "Even after rescuing Keller, he's yet to authorize any of his forces to help us."

"If the emperor's taken out of the equation, and the fallout's significant, it may be all it takes to prove to the Bolarans what an alliance can achieve."

Logan went quiet and turned away from him.

"Your mind's on Novikova."

"Is it that obvious?" Logan retorted.

"I don't know whether it's Sutter or Logan I'm interpreting, but yes, it's like reading a book." Vernon coughed, doing his best to keep the tickle at the bottom of his throat. "You're not coming with us, are you?"

Logan remained silent for several moments. "I have to go back to the Rim."

Vernon nodded as more memories of the past flowed through him. "I suppose if I were you, I'd make that choice, too."

NINETEEN

Novikova sat on the opposite side of Captain Pollock's desk, remaining deathly silent. It was as if she'd been sent to the principal's office. If she was back on the *Ringwood*, she'd have already made half a dozen wisecracks at Estrada's expense. But the *Defender* was a very different place. In such a short space of time, Novikova had gone from a green recruit to being in the company of the most important person on the ship.

How could she be James Sutter?

Trimurilene was foolproof. Lying was impossible. Even if the pilot somehow figured out a way to counteract it, why would she claim to be the Red Hawk when everyone knew Nathan Logan was the true Sutter? Or at least was.

"Bridge to the captain."

Pollock activated the intercom at his fingertips. "Go ahead."

"Sir, we're receiving a transmission from the leadership," an officer from the bridge informed him.

"I'll take it in here."

The lighting inside the office dimmed, and a holographic representation came to life next to Novikova. *"Captain Pollock,"* the man greeted him.

The *Defender's* CO nodded at the projection. "Sir."

The hologram looked at Novikova. Even with heavier eyelids and a slightly more pronounced slouch, the figure was unmistakable. *"Jana Novikova, I see you've joined our ranks."*

She smiled weakly at Fox, recalling the experiences she'd shared with the head of the ORC leadership. The wise beacon of hope still exuded a charisma that was hard to fake, but even he seemed fatigued at what was transpiring.

"My deepest condolences to you," he continued. *"Gelbrana's an integral part of the Outer Rim, and its people some of the staunchest warriors in our rebellion."* He paused, almost lost for words. *"They will forever be in my heart."*

She bowed her head, thanking him for his kind thoughts.

He returned his attention to Pollock. *"We've read your reports on the attack in the Metra Star System, and we've also analyzed the flight recorder salvaged from the patrol ship's debris. It would seem they were attacked by a single Arcadian light carrier, with a complement of five fighters."*

Fox dematerialized, and a holographic representation of the ambush appeared. The cylindrical scope outpost was in a geostationary orbit of the purple gas giant, while the corvette kept its distance at its perimeter.

Then the fireworks began.

The Arcadian light carrier came out of hyperwarp beyond the planet and scrambled its five fighters toward the corvette. Weapon fire was exchanged by all parties, including the outpost, which launched and exhausted its defensive arsenal. The rebels put up an admirable fight, but eventually the highly maneuverable Arcadian fighters won the day, destroying the outpost and then taking down the corvette. The hologram of the skirmish dematerialized, and the older man's image reappeared before them. Fox placed his hands behind his back and regarded them both.

"After being informed of your initial interrogation, we analyzed the movements of your prisoner's fighter before its destruction. From what we can determine, the pilot in your brig is, in fact, James Sutter."

"That makes no sense," Novikova blurted out.

"We completely agree, but there's no doubt from our observations that she flew the same maneuvers we'd expect the Red Hawk to fly in a similar scenario, and with the same skillset."

"Couldn't that be trained? Surely Sutter's campaigns are taught at the academy."

"Every individual pilot has certain ticks. Sutter's aren't overly obvious because of the smoothness in which he flies, but they're there. And she had them. They were identical." Fox paused. *"What's worrying is she wasn't the only pilot to exhibit these ticks."*

"You're saying the other four had them, too?" Pollock asked.

Fox nodded. *"Our analysts have concluded they all displayed signs of Sutter's flying style."*

"For the love of the gods," Novikova muttered. "Artemis Unit's still operating."

Fox held his gaze on Novikova. "This does appear to have Artemis' fingerprints all over it."

Novikova remembered the day Logan had come back from his mission to destroy the outpost in the Dylaria Star System. The mission had been a success. At least that's what everyone thought. "They survived then..."

"That's the conclusion we've come to," Fox said. *"One*

must assume Artemis has devised a way to replicate Sutter's experiences so they can place them into the mind of other individuals."

Captain Pollock strummed his fingers on the desk. "If what you say is true, then the Arcadians potentially have squadrons of James Sutters out there."

A lump formed in Novikova's throat. Not only at the possibility of the Empire having such an overriding advantage, but also at the thought that what made Logan who he was could be so easily replicated.

"We're already facing increased difficulties since the destruction of Gelbrana with the Empire's push toward the Rim's core worlds," Fox declared. "But if what we've discovered is true, it would make the Arcadians' fighters almost unbeatable in battle."

The terrifying reality of their situation permeated through the office. "What are our orders, sir?" Pollock asked.

"I want you to go back to your brig and interrogate what's left of your prisoner." The thoughtful old man had been replaced with a youthful decisiveness. "We have to know where Artemis Unit is. If there are more James Sutters out there, as we can be fairly certain there are, we need to have Artemis Unit's new location."

"Aye, sir."

"Good luck." Fox's holographic form shimmered from existence, and the office's lights went back to their normal level of illumination.

Pollock jumped from his seat and made his way to the door. "Come on, recruit. I'd like you with me on this one."

TWENTY

The sickbay of the *Defender* was warm compared to the medical bay on the *Ringwood*. For some reason, Doctor Sachdev preferred working in an environment with the same temperature as a meat locker. Novikova could only assume it was because the surgeon was a native of Antar Colony. While she'd never visited the planet, tales existed of how unbearably cold their winters could be for off-worlders. Even though the destroyer's sickbay was more comfortable, there was still a distinct chill in the air.

When Captain Pollock led her inside, the *Defender's* CMO had already strapped the Arcadian pilot to the main bed in the center of the room. The flowing red hair of the person claiming to be James Sutter was tied back and her eyes closed. Novikova wondered how alive the woman truly was. Legend had it that those treated with trimurilene went through a bevy of different experiences. Not only was the brain torn apart, piece by piece, but it broke an individual to the point where nothing inside could be repaired. Apparently, at the end, it was like an out-of-body experience where you could only watch yourself betray those you'd given your allegiance to.

Novikova looked around for the ship's doctor, but he'd

already left. She wondered if it had anything to do with his medical values opposing what was about to happen. There instead was the *Defender's* chief security officer, Commander Henson. The stern woman was quite tall but also physically fitter than Novikova could ever hope to be.

"Has the doctor given you the bevanox, Commander?" Pollock asked her.

Henson revealed the syringe in her hand. "He's set the dosage for me."

"Good." The captain cleared his throat. "Do it."

Henson put the needle into pilot's arm. Nothing happened at first, and the pilot's eyes remained closed. But then one of her legs twitched. Followed by another. Eventually, both the Arcadian's eyelids wavered. The trimurilene had likely done so much damage, she probably didn't know where she was or how she'd got there. That's why they'd given her the bevanox. It was the only drug that could effectively bring her back for that little bit longer.

"Captain Sutter, can you hear me?" Pollock asked.

The pilot didn't reply.

Henson put a hand on her shoulder and shook her. Drool dripped from Arcadian's mouth along with some slurred words.

Pollock leaned closer. "You'll need to repeat that."

"I...can...hear...you..." she said.

"Can you confirm you are Captain James Sutter?"

The pilot nodded ever so slowly. "Yes."

Novikova got distracted by the slow heartbeat of the prisoner coming from the vitals monitor on the other side of the bed. She knew little about medicine, but even she realized at the rate at which the woman's heart was beating, she didn't have long.

"How?" Pollock pressed, moving closer so she could hear him.

The pilot tilted her head. "How...what?"

"How can you be James Sutter? Sutter's a man. You're a woman."

Novikova thought for a moment she saw the pilot grin, but it was just her lips squirming with more drool dripping from its edge.

"There...are...several...of...us."

"How many? How many James Sutters are out there?"

"Dozens... Hundreds... Thousands."

Pollock glared at Henson and put his hand by the side of the prisoner's head. "But how?"

The pilot opened her mouth to speak, but nothing came out. On the monitor, her heart rate spiked, and she flopped under the strength of the restraints.

"Inject her again!" Pollock wailed at his chief of security.

Henson complied and gave her another dose of the bevanox. Her body slowly calmed, and her heart rate returned to some normality.

"We have to know how the Empire's creating multiple James Sutters," Pollock said.

The Arcadian quivered. "Art...e...mis."

Novikova sighed. Fox was right. Artemis Unit was still out there, continuing to develop ways of bringing down the Outer Rim and the rest of its enemies.

"Were you 'created' at Artemis?" the captain continued.

She nodded. "Yes."

"Do you know where Artemis is?"

"Yes."

"Where?"

Her almost dead eyes looked into his.

"Where, dammit!" he snapped.

"A...station."

"Where?"

"Cor..."

"Cor?" He glanced at Henson. "Cor?"

"Vair," the pilot said.

Novikova walked to the side of the bed. "The Corvair Star System?"

Realization came over the captain's features, and he refocused back on the prisoner. "Where in the Corvair Star System?"

"The..." The pilot's speech became even more garbled. "Fifth...plan—"

The Arcadian's heart rate went through the roof again, and she convulsed, flailing about in the bed. Novikova instinctively moved backward. For a moment she thought Pollock was going to tell Henson to inject her with more bevanox. But he stopped himself. The woman might have been the enemy. She may have even been James Sutter in some twisted way. But she'd been through enough.

The prisoner finally stopped quaking, and the heart rate turned into a long whine. Henson put a hand on her chest to check if she was still breathing and shook her head at the captain, closing over her eyelids. There might have been several James Sutters out there, however, this one was now very much dead.

TWENTY-ONE

Vernon stepped into the cockpit as the *Corina II* pulled out of hyperwarp. She entered the orbit of Garvin IX high above the shadowy world. Once upon a time, the industrial planet was a stop-off point for Arcadian forces before they left for Bolar or Thandeea. It was an integral part of the supply line between the Empire and its territories on the fringe. But since they'd brought the two worlds under the emperor's rule, Garvin had resumed being a mostly civilian operation.

"That cloud layer's a little thicker from the last time I was here," he commented at the brown haze swirling in the atmosphere, blocking out a view of the land and oceans below.

"Last time Sutter was here, it was a navigational nightmare," Logan said from the helm. "You better take a seat."

Vernon took his advice and sat next to him at the copilot's station, doing his best not to cough up his lungs. Just gazing out at the awful environmental conditions made him sick. Arcadia would likely have looked similar if it wasn't for its expansive weather networks. The Arcadians lived to such an excess that the technology integrated into their society had the ability shield them from what they were really doing to their planet. It was the sacrifices of places like Garvin IX that kept their world an idyllic paradise.

The *Corina II* entered the atmosphere and shook from the foreign elements expelled by the factories deep below. Everything around them darkened, and the vessel pushed through the cloud layers. It was almost as if Logan was piloting them through a nebula. Eventually, the quaking subsided, and they emerged on the other side. What appeared, though, didn't fill Vernon's senses with joy. Since his last visit, the density of Garvin IX's capital city had exploded. The factories and other production facilities had continued to sprawl out in every direction. Vernon pitied those who lived and worked down there. He could only ponder how many years it took off their lives.

Logan sat higher in his seat to get a lay of the land and checked his scopes. "Seems the spaceport's beyond the city center." He navigated them down carefully, maneuvering through the busy traffic above the buildings. He continued on through some tall skyscrapers until a huge ovular complex appeared ahead.

Vernon requested a docking permit, and it was promptly received via the comms. In his typical cavalier fashion, Logan brought them down rapidly and slowed at the last second, before touching down.

Vernon glared at him and heaved himself up, following him through the exit to the ship's airlock where Alira, Keller, and the rest of the Bolarans were waiting. Briggs went to the door and opened it, revealing the crisp breeze so synonymous with the planet. The soldiers made their way inside the spaceport, while Logan, Vernon, Keller, and Alira remained at the top of the ramp.

"I guess I can't convince you to come with us?" Keller asked Logan.

He shook his head. "The Rim's calling."

"I never expected the Red Hawk to run from a fight."

Logan scowled. "There's more fights that need to be won."

"Yes, I suppose there are." The Bolaran stepped closer to him and put out his hand. "Maybe by some miracle we'll meet again. If not, I'm sure I'll see you in the depths of the afterlife."

Logan stared at his hand and shook it. Keller headed down the ramp, and Alira nodded her appreciation, following him.

"Well, it seems this is goodbye." Logan dove into his top pocket and yanked out Vernon's father's dog tags. "I know you said I could keep these, but you probably need them more than I do where you're heading."

Vernon picked them up and read his father's name, which had become barely legible with its age. The spirit of his dad swirled inside him. "Thank you."

Logan pointed to the ship. "Well, I better go."

"Don't hang about here too long. Head out of Arcadian space and don't look back."

Before he knew it, Logan threw his arms around him, forcing his muscles to clench from the expression of affection. "Say hello to the emperor for me."

"I'll make sure of it."

Logan eased himself away and entered the ship.

"Hey," Vernon said, clearing his throat.

Logan stopped. "Yeah?"

Vernon tried to find the words. "Nothing. Just don't get too cocky out there."

Logan mock saluted and closed the airlock, giving him one last wave. Vernon edged backward, and the vessel prepared to launch.

Alira approached Vernon from the behind. "What were you going to tell him?"

"Hmm?"

The *Corina II's* ventral thrusters powered up, and the craft slowly lifted off the ground.

"Oh." Vernon put his hand over his mouth and coughed, leaving some sprays of blood in his palm. "I've got Makriak's Disease. I wanted to tell him I'm never going to see him again."

Logan piloted the ship upward, and it pushed into the air, disappearing amongst Garvin IX's dark clouds.

"But I figured what's the point." Vernon took out a handkerchief from his pocket and wiped his hand. "It's not like any of us are coming back from this mission anyway."

TWENTY-TWO

Admiral Jones stared through the viewport of his office as the *Imperator* churned toward the massive gas giant designated Yaringal VI. It's mostly nitrogen-methane atmosphere caused it to glow a radiant neon green. He'd rarely seen anything so spectacular. It had been many years since he'd traveled so deep into the Outer Rim, considering the bulk of his career was spent either on patrol or in direct conflict with the Bolarans and Thandeeans. Every light-year the *Imperator* gained in the Rim contained something new and different but also represented the nearing conclusion of a war he so desperately wanted to end.

On the sill beneath him sat two cigars, with red rings wrapped around them. They were from the finest growers on Jontoria and were one of the most sought-after items anywhere in the Empire. Nothing came close to their smoothness or full flavor. Councilor McCrae had gifted him a box when he'd made Jones an admiral, and slowly but surely, he'd smoked his way through most of them. The pair in front of him were the last ones remaining.

His door chime sounded, and he rubbed his eyes, pushing aside his fatigue. "Come."

The door opened, and a junior officer from the bridge entered. Jones cast his gaze at the man through the reflection of the viewport.

"The reports you requested, sir," he said, holding a data pad in front of him.

"Read them out to me, Ensign," Jones instructed him.

"Uh, which one?"

"Just start at the top."

"Uh, yes, sir." The ensign activated the pad. "The ninth fleet report they've wiped out ORC resistance near the seventh planet of the Teratar Star System. They're currently on course to the third to investigate—"

"Next."

"Umm, the seventh fleet have recorded heavy casualties at the Horsario Nebula, but they believe they've uncovered a secret ORC operation."

Jones turned. "As I suspected. Instruct comms to send a communiqué to Admiral Papopolos and ask him if he requires any assistance."

The ensign tapped the note on his pad. "Aye, sir."

"Anything else?"

"Yes, we've received word from the light carrier *Blood Spear* that they've destroyed an ORC scope outpost in the Metra Star System along with a patrol corvette which was guarding it. They've reported—"

Jones reached over his desk and yanked the pad from the junior officer's hand. He checked it and plonked it next to the control panel on his desk. The lights dimmed, and a holographic projection appeared, revealing the full skirmish of the *Blood Spear* and its squadron of James Sutters going up against ORC forces. The fighters moving in sync was artistry, and the destruction of the enemy their bloody canvas. "You were about to tell me something, Ensign?"

"Yes, sir. It was reported even though the mission was a success, one pilot's fighter was destroyed."

"That's unfortunate."

There was an explosion on the particular craft's wing, and what appeared to be the pilot ejecting from their craft.

"Were they recovered? Jones asked.

"No. It would seem…"

"Well, spit it out, Ensign."

"The *Blood Spear's* informed us an ORC destroyer moved into the star system after they left. It's believed they may have captured our pilot."

Jones eyed the ejected 'Sutter' in the projection and picked up the pad. It deactivated the hologram, and he threw it at the ensign, who skillfully plucked it from the air. "That'll be all."

"There's more here, sir."

"I said that will be all." He returned his attention to the viewport and watched the ensign leave the office through the reflection. Jones picked up the cigars and twirled them in his fingers.

Vernon couldn't say whether it was night or day on the streets of Garvin IX. With such thick cloud cover, it was impossible to know if it was the sun or one of the planet's three moons above his head. He'd visited some shoddy places in his time, but there was something so awful about the industrial world that made him wish he was back on Cantabria Colony, shooting it out with the desert mafia Logan had got himself involved with.

Keller led him and Alira down the street, but Vernon remained a few steps behind them, letting them catch up with one another. He wasn't sure what their relationship entailed, but there was definitely a romantic element to it. Or as romantic as possible between those who headed a rebellion. He'd never forgotten the propaganda fed to him when he was an Arcadian pilot. The Bolarans were portrayed as sub-human. A bastard element. And while he'd concluded over time they weren't the barbarians they'd been painted to be, they were still a very strange people.

The trio continued around the next corner into a dark alley, where the ground was soaked from the rain that had greeted them when they'd left the spaceport. The smell of garbage and urine wafted through the air, nearly making Vernon barf. He did his best to hold his breath and stopped with the others at a door.

Keller pounded his fist on it in an unusual sequence.

No one answered.

Just as he was about to do it again, the door creaked open. The Bolaran man entered first, and Alira followed. Vernon stepped warily over the threshold behind them. Inside, hundreds, if not thousands of cargo containers were stacked to the ceiling. None had any labels, but Vernon had visited enough similar haunts in his lifetime to realize they were filled with contraband.

"I never thought I'd see you again!" a voice boomed from out of nowhere.

They looked in every direction to try to find its owner, but the enormous warehouse was empty. A chill ran down Vernon's back, and a huge door clunked open at the far end of the storeroom. A man, at least a foot shorter than Keller, emerged from the shadows and walked up to them. His expression was grim. Eventually, a smarmy smile appeared.

"You look like hell," he said to the Bolaran leader. "What happened to you?"

"Long story," Keller told him. "It's good to see you, Bodan."

The trader stepped in front of Alira and sized her up. "You... you're much prettier." He took her hand to kiss it, but she twisted his arm and screwed him around.

He howled in agony and chuckled. "You're a feisty one, aren't you?"

She let go of him, and he pressed out the creases in his shirt.

"I should've guessed you'd bring a firecracker with you, Keller." Bodan moved on to Vernon. "Where did you get this fossil?"

Vernon wanted to try and break his arm, too. He thought better of it. He didn't have Alira's beauty to stop Bodan from striking back, or the youth or health to put up a fight.

Bodan went back to Keller and placed his hands on his hips. "So, what brings you to Garvin? I didn't think I'd see you again after the Empire started tightening their patrols between here and Bolar."

"Getting here wasn't a problem this time around. The Arcadians have bigger fish to fry at the moment," Keller said. "I will, however, require your help to leave."

"You need a ship?"

"I need a ship."

"That's easy. I've got plenty. It just depends what kind and how much you want to spend."

"It has to be an Arcadian ship."

"Most of what I have are civilian-built Arcadian vessels."

"I'm not talking about a civilian craft."

Bodan's eyes widened. "Oh."

"Can you help me?" Keller asked.

"An Arcadian military vessel." The trader rubbed his chin. "Yeah, I guess so, but it'll cost you."

"Show me what you've got."

Bodan led them to the door of the storeroom, and they hopped inside an old elevator. It dropped with some serious speed. Vernon couldn't tell how far they dived, but he suspected wherever he was headed, it was once a mine shaft. When they arrived, the trader pushed the rusty door aside and invited them out.

"After you, my dear," he said to Alira, who took up the offer and led them into a dimly lit corridor.

Vernon coughed from what little oxygen there was and followed everyone through an archway, fashioned from the rock, into a cramped flight deck. Bodan flipped a switch, and a series of bright lights flickered to life, revealing a single craft at its center.

"A K2-Class transport?" Vernon muttered. "They stopped building these twenty years ago."

"That's right," the Garvinian said. "There's still a few kicking around after all this time."

"Something this old might put a target on our back," Alira added.

"I've updated it with all the current Empire codes. It may not be pretty, but it'll get you where you need to go."

Keller banged on the hull with his fist. "How much are you asking?"

Bodan took a data pad from his pocket and handed it to him.

Keller whistled. "That's pretty steep."

"You'd be buying a genuine Arcadian military craft. Just getting my hands on it was a miracle, and bringing it up to spec was a nightmare. I can't accept anything less than that."

Keller waved Alira over to him. "Very well. We'll take it."

The Bolaran woman pulled a cable from her jacket and plugged it into his neck port, attaching the other end into the pad.

"I wasn't expecting that," the trader quipped as the transaction was completed. "I hope you know how to pilot this thing. She's not as agile as the newer stuff coming off the production line these days."

"I know how to pilot it."

Bodan and the Bolarans turned to Vernon, stepping forward.

"At least I used to a long time ago," he told them.

TWENTY-THREE

"Take us out of hyperwarp, recruit."

Novikova pressed in the commands on the helm, following her captain's orders and gliding the *Defender* into sub-light. The contorted stars of faster-than-light speed disappeared and were replaced with the deep abyss of space. Lieutenant Reimer nodded his satisfaction with the maneuver next to her, and a silence fell over the bridge as everyone waited.

"Anything?" Pollock asked Ensign Georgiou.

The officer checked his readings. "I'm picking up a vessel on an intercept course. The ID transponder matches the code the leadership have provided us."

There was an audible sigh amongst the officers at their stations. No one enjoyed being out in open space, or ambush-territory, as it was colloquially known. The sooner their rendezvous was over with the better. A spark of light soon appeared beyond their position, and the vessel from the scopes emerged from hyperwarp. At first it was but a small gray speck, but as it neared, it took a familiar shape. Novikova did her best not to appear surprised. Or excited.

"They're hailing," came the call from the *Defender's* communications officer.

"Let's hear it," Pollock instructed her.

"ORC Defender, *this is Nathan Logan, requesting permission to dock."*

Novikova beamed, and a tingle ran through her from top to bottom.

"Permission granted," Pollock said.

Novikova stood from her station. "Sir?"

"Recruit?"

"Request permission to welcome our liaison from the leadership aboard." She realized she was making a spectacle of herself, as well as being incredibly presumptuous. She frankly didn't care.

Pollock gave her a knowing look. "Lieutenant, take the helm."

Reimer relieved Novikova, and she strode casually to the exit. Once she was off the bridge and out of the captain's sight, she scampered to the elevator. On the docking deck, she weaved through a team of engineers and techs going about their work, until finally reaching the airlock.

The light flashed green, and the door slid open, revealing a shadowy figure inside. He stepped into the light, and a tingle again flowed through Novikova's body.

Logan's mouth dropped. "Jana?"

She wrapped her arms around him, and he took hold of her, lifting her into the air. Their lips met, and for a moment she found herself lost in another place at another time. He eventually put her down, and she caught a glimpse of the three infantry recruits who'd come along with her from the *Liberty Cry*. They stopped in the middle of the corridor and watched on with amusement.

"Pitts! Prior! Singh! Move!" Their sergeant appeared behind them and quickly nudged them on, much to their chagrin.

"You're the last person I expected to see here. What

happened on Bolar? Did you secure an alliance?" Novikova gazed past him into the *Corina II*. "Where's Vernon?"

"It's all a very long story." He put his hands on her shoulders. "You've already been to Gelbrana, haven't you?"

She closed her eyes and pushed back the tears. He held her again, and she nuzzled into his shoulder. "They're all gone..."

Logan didn't let her go.

"They burned it. They burned it all." The memories of the flattened corn fields, her smoldering home, and the remains of her parents flooded back to her all at once.

Logan pushed aside her fringe and kissed her on the forehead. "I'm so sorry, Jana."

Logan made his way to the head of the table and took a seat. Captain Pollock and his XO, Commander Emovic, sat at the other opposite him, while the chief of security was seated to his left with the ship's CMO. Lieutenant Reimer, the *Defender's* helm officer, took a position at his right.

Logan wished Novikova was there with him. He'd only got to see her for the barest of moments when he'd arrived, but with her rank not yet recognized in the chain of command, it would've been a hard sell getting her involved. Even with the mission on his mind, he was still trying to compute seeing her in an ORC uniform. From the moment he'd met her on Brindara, he understood the tightrope she walked between the guilt of not joining the fight and the devotion she had for her parents. Obviously, with the attacks on Gelbrana, things had changed immensely.

"Is everyone here?" he asked Pollock.

The captain nodded, and Logan dimmed the lights, activating the briefing room's holographic projector. A star chart appeared, with twelve planets orbiting its sun.

"This is the Corvair Star System. It's located at what was once the soft border between the Outer Rim and the rest of the Arcadian Empire." He zoomed in on the fifth planet. "And here, if the information your prisoner provided is correct, is Artemis Unit's new location."

Anger had been simmering inside him since being informed of Artemis Unit's resurrection. Unfortunately, he wasn't surprised. When he'd led the attack on the original base in the Dylaria Star System, the Arcadians had been waiting. They'd known he was coming and likely evacuated much of the facility before it was destroyed. What he hadn't expected was to come face to face with reports of their new weapon. The thought of more James Sutters out there terrified him no end.

"What are our orders?" Pollock asked.

"At this stage, recon only," Logan said. "With most of our forces pressed back into the Rim, we're to fly into Corvair, get as close to the base as we can, take a few snaps, and hightail it out of there. However..."

"However?"

"If we believe we have the ability to destroy Artemis, we're to do so."

"And the potential dangers?"

"Difficult to say." Logan frowned. "No scans of the system have been taken since the front line moved closer to the Rim's core. It could be heavily fortified or be guarded by sporadic patrols. We just don't know."

Pollock shifted uncomfortably in his chair and turned

to Reimer. "What's the safest trajectory into Corvair, Lieutenant?"

Reimer rubbed his chin and pointed at the gas giants making up the outer part of the system. "I'd suggest staying close to these planets until we can safely make our way to the fifth planet."

"Sounds like a good old-fashioned game of hide and seek," Emovic quipped.

"I agree with the lieutenant," Logan said.

"Why do you think the Arcadians have based Artemis so close to the front?"

The same question had lingered in Logan's mind ever since his own briefing on his return from Garvin IX by the leadership. "One must assume if they're 'replicating' James Sutters, they'd want the facility near the Rim so they can deploy their pilots quickly."

The *Defender's* captain tapped his fingers against the table. His contemplative stare was one Logan knew only too well. He wondered if he was better off staying with Vernon. But then he thought about all the potential pilots out there, resembling the monster inside him.

"Okay then." Pollock stood. "Lieutenant Reimer, set a course for the Corvair Star System."

TWENTY-FOUR

The beams on the ceiling shimmered as the *Defender* propelled through hyperwarp, the glow of the stars rippling throughout Novikova's quarters.

The clock on the table next to her read oh-four-hundred. She hadn't got a wink of sleep for the entire night. Or any night since she'd arrived on the ORC ship. At first, she wondered if it was because she was out of her comfort zone aboard the military vessel, or perhaps she wasn't used to her new bed. In her heart of hearts, though, she knew exactly the reason. And no amount of time could heal the wounds of what she'd left behind.

Logan rolled over next to her, and his eyes blinked open. "You're still awake?"

She smiled weakly. "I'm obviously not the only one."

"Too much on my mind."

"Tell me about it."

He sat up and checked the clock. "Aren't you supposed to be up at six?"

Novikova nodded. "Reimer wants me to do some assessments on the simulator."

"You're going to be exhausted."

"And whose fault's that?" She leaned over and kissed him gently.

"Sure, blame the new guy."

Novikova wrapped her arms around him. "You're thinking about Vernon, aren't you?"

He dragged the sheet over him and dropped his head on the stiff pillow. "He's old enough and ugly enough to look after himself."

When Logan had arrived, he'd told her little about the mission. While he'd explained everything that had happened when they'd gone to Bolar and the subsequent rescue of Michael Keller, he had to omit the rest. And deliberately so, by order of the ORC leadership. She had no idea what Vernon was doing with the Bolarans, but it was obviously important. And probably extremely dangerous.

Logan craned his neck and took her hand, clasping it tight. His thoughts might have been someplace else, but there was calmness in his features. Ironically, it was likely the part of him that was James Sutter that gave him that strength.

You don't become a hero of the Empire without keeping your wits in a crisis.

That's what made it that much scarier. Novikova had already seen firsthand what the new Arcadian pilots were capable of. If more Sutters were to be unleashed, the war would be over quicker than anyone imagined. For the Rim, it would be a nightmare scenario.

"How does this all end, Logan?"

He pulled himself from his trance-like state and snuck a look at the clock. "You need to get some sleep, Jana."

It wasn't the answer she wanted, even if it was the one she needed to hear.

Another Sutter trait, no doubt.

She rolled over, and he edged closer to her, putting an

arm over her shoulder. The warmth of his body radiated through her, and she closed her eyes once more.

Before she knew it, her alarm sounded.

———

Vernon walked to the coffee dispenser inside the kitchen facility of their new ship, the *Night Cutter*, and leaned on the counter. The confined space was even tighter than that of the *Corina II*. Thankfully, no one else was there to get in his way.

He scrounged for a mug, but there were none in the cupboards above or beneath him. He checked the sink to find a green ceramic cup with a chip in it, likely left by one of the Bolaran soldiers. With some hot water, he rinsed it and took it over to the dispenser, thumbing in his order. The brown liquid poured into the mug, and he had a sip. He spluttered and hacked his way through a coughing fit. He keeled over and rode it out until the sensation in his throat finally let up.

"The coffee can't be that bad."

He turned to Keller, stepping over the threshold, leaving little room to move in the kitchenette. "Or is it the Makriak's Disease?"

Vernon found a napkin and wiped his mouth. He scrunched up the soft tissue with large blotches of blood on it and threw it in the trash can. "So, she told you?"

"Of course. Alira tells me everything."

"The coughing apparently gets pretty bad at this point." Vernon had another sip of his coffee. "This stuff doesn't help either. I don't suppose you can plug yourself into the dispenser and reprogram it, can you?"

Keller chuckled. "I probably could, but I think I'll save my energy."

"A pity." Vernon put the bitter drink down and crossed his arms, facing the Bolaran.

"You so desperately want to ask the question."

"Do I?"

"You want to know why I did this to myself."

"I know why you did it. It's the same reason we do all the things we do in this business." Vernon cleared his throat of any lingering discomfort. "How, uh, how long—"

"How long until these things under my skin kill me?"

Vernon nodded.

Keller looked past him for a moment. "No one's ever done this before, so I'm not sure. But every day a new part of me aches. Every day more skin flakes away, and soon I'll be lucky to have any of the dozen hairs left on my head. If I can see out this mission and put a bullet through the emperor's head, I'll be happy to leave this world."

Vernon couldn't fault him for his gusto. If he'd had a similar opportunity, he'd have probably done the same. As it stood, they were both dying. Both were being eaten from the inside out.

"I suppose at least I'll die for a worthwhile reason," Keller said.

"What's that supposed to mean?" Vernon asked.

"I know how one gets Makriak's Disease. It's from retrium radiation. The retrium found in the power core of old D-Class two-seater fighters. They would've been pulled from service decades ago around the time you were training in the Arcadian Fighter Corps. For some, the disease festers away for years until finally reaching the surface. I suppose you've had a good run. Ultimately, that's the difference between you and me. I'll have sacrificed for the cause. You'll just shrivel away because as a younger man you decided to fly the flag of the Empire."

"I actually never flew in the old D-Class."

Keller raised his eyebrows.

Vernon picked up his coffee and took another taste of the awful brew. "When fighting broke out in the Outer Rim, and the ORC claimed a series of early victories against the Arcadians, every kid from colonies enlisted, wanting to give the Empire a kick in the teeth. There were more pilots than fighters. Training wasn't easy, so we had to instruct them in anything we could get our hands on. I taught hundreds of recruits in old E-Class and F-Class wrecks that'd been rusting away. Unbeknownst to us at the time, one of those fighters had a retrium power core inside it. That was only a year ago. Unfortunately for me, the disease didn't take long to fester."

Keller said nothing. It seemed all the advanced synthetic processors in his pathetic body couldn't devise a response.

"When you're taking your shot at the emperor," Vernon said, brushing by him, "I'll make sure not to let my flag get in the way."

TWENTY-FIVE

Logan hadn't moved. Not even an inch.

It was more than he could say for the ship's captain, who hadn't stopped prowling between the port and starboard sides of the bridge since their arrival. Past him at the helm, Novikova stood next to Lieutenant Reimer as the *Defender* slowly made its way to the fifth planet of the Corvair Star System. So far, they'd been in the clear. Nothing had appeared on the scopes when they'd pulled out of hyperwarp apart from some errant space dust.

Hopping from planet to planet was slow going, using the large gas giants of the outer part of the system to shield themselves from any ambush. An anxiety lingered in the air. No matter how young some of the officers were, they'd been at war long enough to know what could lurk around the next corner.

"We're coming out from behind the sixth planet, Captain," Reimer informed his CO from the helm.

Pollock stopped in the middle of the bridge next to Commander Emovic. The massive red gas giant disappeared to port, and open space again took center stage. "Anything?" he asked Georgiou at the scopes.

Georgiou examined the readings and shook his head. "It appears we have a clear path through to Corvair V."

Pollock glanced back at Logan but quickly turned away when their eyes met. Logan wasn't sure what the *Defender's* captain thought of him. His reception hadn't exactly been frosty, but it was certainly guarded. He'd likely heard all the stories. No matter where Logan went, the shadow of the Red Hawk always hung over him.

Time seemed to slow as they continued toward their target. Logan remembered back to when he was James Sutter. Nothing bothered the Arcadian pilot more than long missions sitting on his ass in his fighter. Even though he was one of the best to take their place in a cockpit, he always feared boredom, worried any kind of complacency would be his downfall.

"Approaching the fifth planet, sir," came the call from the helm.

Novikova looked behind her at Logan, who still hadn't moved, doing what he could to stay out of everyone's way. They exchanged wary smiles with one another before she returned her attention to her duties. Beyond her, the green orb of Corvair V became larger, along with its solitary moon. While Logan had never been to the world, he was well-versed in its geography. It was the only planet remotely inhabitable in the entire system. But even that was a stretch. It might have seemed like a tropical paradise from above, but its atmosphere was heavily concentrated with carbon dioxide, making it a little uncomfortable for human life.

Commander Emovic made his way to the helm and instructed Reimer to take them into orbit. Pollock went over to Ensign Georgiou, telling him to commence intensive scans of the area. Everyone remained silent while the ship rounded the planet on the hunt for Artemis Unit's new home.

"I'm getting nothing," Georgiou said. "There's no made-made objects in orbit anywhere."

"What about on the surface?" Pollock asked. "The Arcadian pilot was so drugged-up, her information might've been inaccurate."

The younger officer rechecked his scopes. "No, sir. The board's clear."

Pollock spun around again. This time, though, his eyes didn't waver from Logan. "It's a trap!"

A lump formed in Logan's throat. From the moment the mission was explained to him, there was always a possibility of the Arcadians pulling such a move, but he and the leadership judged it unlikely. With the Empire continuing to press at the front lines, it made no sense to focus their efforts on such a small ambush operation.

Unless this is something else...

Logan didn't have time to ponder. The bridge of the *Defender* turned into a frenzy of activity with the command team shouting their orders to every corner. Junior officers liaised with their teams below deck over the comms, and red lights filtered from the ceiling, signifying the activation of the combat systems.

"We need to get out of here now!" Pollock barked.

"I'm on it, sir," Reimer said, punching in an escape course.

Emovic rubbed his chin, holding his position next to the ship's combat officer. "Where the hell could they be hiding?"

The *Defender* pushed away from Corvair V, and the planet's moon appeared in their path. Before he could utter another word, an Arcadian carrier revealed itself from behind the moon. Alarms blared across the bridge, and the voices of the crew intensified as they spoke over the top of each other, preparing for the engagement.

Pollock rushed to the helm. "Lieutenant Reimer, take us about and return to the planet. Calculate another course out of here."

"Aye, sir," came the reply.

"Ready all aft defensive batteries," Emovic told the combat officer. "Communications, send a distress call, informing any friendlies that we've been ambushed."

"I can't broadcast anything out of here, Commander." The communications officer swiveled around. "The Arcadians are jamming us."

"Sir, they're preparing to fire!" Georgiou interrupted.

Pollock and Emovic stared at one another. Logan and Novikova joined them.

A series of bleeps sounded from the scopes, indicating the launched missiles. Logan finally moved and went over to the combat station next to the *Defender's* XO. The destroyer was much more agile than the carrier, but in such an open area of space, the smaller vessel would be unable to use its advantage.

"Target the incoming missiles. Keep the heat off our tail," Pollock ordered. "Helm, prepare for evasive maneuvers."

The two younger officers acknowledged his commands in unison, and the *Defender* fired its countermeasures. On the combat monitor, dots representing the missiles converged and made contact. None of the carrier's volley made it through, but the space between the combatants quaked from the explosions. The hull of the destroyer reverberated, shaking the deck beneath everyone's feet.

"Lieutenant, I need a course out of here," Pollock repeated to his helmsman.

Before Reimer could respond, more missiles propelled from the weapon tubes of the Arcadian carrier. Another series of alarms wailed, and the XO gave the countermeasure order. The arsenals of the two vessels met again, lighting up the cosmos above the insignificant jungle world.

"Two have got through!" Georgiou yelled from the opposite side of the bridge.

Reimer did the best he could to evade. Unfortunately, the missiles were too quick for his reflexes. A pair of almighty booms sounded, and the *Defender* lurched forward, sending those on their feet sprawling to the deck. Logan went down with a thud next to Commander Emovic, and the lights flickered above their heads. Novikova careened down near the helm, splattered in a similar position. His heart stopped for a moment at her prone form.

"Jana..."

Her legs eventually got moving, and she planted her hands on the deck to heave herself up. Logan breathed a sigh of relief and got up with help from Emovic.

"Captain," Reimer said. "That shot took out our hyperwarp capability and main thruster assembly."

"Not to mention our aft missile tubes," the combat officer told him.

Pollock instinctively turned to the scopes, where Georgiou shook his head.

"The carrier's closing in, sir," he said to the CO as silence again permeated across the bridge.

Logan furrowed his brow. "They're not firing..."

"They've got us on a platter," Emovic added, as surprised as him. "What are they waiting for?"

"Wait a second." Georgiou checked his monitors.

"They're scrambling jumpships along with a fighter escort."

"Not exactly standard Arcadian operating procedure."

Logan rubbed his sweaty hands on his pants. As Georgiou had claimed, the bogeys of the intercepting crafts appeared on the combat monitor.

He put two and two together.

"Uh-oh."

TWENTY-SIX

It might have been thirty years since Vernon had last piloted a K2-Class transport, but it felt like only yesterday.
As a pilot for the Empire, most of his flying was done in
the cockpit of a fighter, but his accreditation also gave him
the ability to take the helm of crafts such as the K2. Usually, it was to transport dignitaries or haul supplies if there
was a personnel shortage.

As it was all those decades earlier, the vessel was a
vastly different beast to handle. Gone were the multiple
thruster options, along with its smaller and lighter frame,
instead replaced with a much bulkier and far heavier hull.
Modern vessels, such as the *Corina*, were a breeze to fly
compared to the antique he was now sitting in.

Some footfalls sounded from the door, and Alira and
Keller entered the *Night Cutter's* cockpit. The command
confines, like the rest of the ship, were a tight prospect.
Finding space for all three of them was a challenge. Alira
took the copilot's seat built into the bulkhead to his right,
while Keller remained behind him, breathing down his
neck with his unbearable wheeze.

"What's our position?" Keller asked.

"I'm preparing to take us out of hyperwarp near Magnus III," Vernon said.

The Bolaran man turned to Alira. "Have you got everything prepared?"

She pressed her keypad and brought up a series of complicated number and letter combinations. "We're ready to go."

Vernon double-checked his navigation screens to ensure a safe exit trajectory and toggled the switches to his right, pulling the ship out of hyperwarp, sailing them out into sub-light. Ahead, the desolate gray rock of Magnus III appeared, its surface temperature registering over three hundred below zero.

Not exactly a resort.

He directed the vessel toward the planet slowly. But just as he was about to enter orbit, a proximity alert wailed.

Keller shot a glance at Alira. "What's happening?"

"Three Arcadian corvettes and a fighter squadron are on an intercept course," she said. "I'm also picking up a destroyer patrol near Magnus III's fourth moon."

"Not to mention the five more battle groups prowling about the system," Vernon added. "We must be in the right place."

Any lingering doubt there was evaporated, and his mind took him back to the one and only time he'd come face to face with the emperor. The Empire's sole leader had been nearing old age back then. He could only wonder what he looked like now.

Would he remember me?

Would he remember those who fought and died for him in his irrelevant wars?

Vernon shook off the ridiculous notions and focused

on the job at hand. He brought the *Night Cutter* to a full stop, and the Arcadians surrounded them.

"The lead ship's hailing," Alira said.

"Put them on," Keller instructed her.

"Transport Night Cutter, *this is Magnus Perimeter Command. Identify yourself and state your intentions."*

Keller placed his hands together and cracked his knuckles. "Magnus Command, I'm Lieutenant Bishop of the Sector Fifteen Tech Division. We're here to perform scheduled maintenance at Magnus III."

"You'll need to transmit your authorization."

"Sending it now." Keller nodded to Alira, and she keyed in the delivery of the orders they'd painstakingly forged from the data downloaded on Deltex V. If it didn't appear authentic, their mission was over before it had begun.

Silence filled the other end of the channel, lasting a little too long for Vernon's liking. He checked the scopes for any way out of orbit. There wasn't the slightest gap anywhere. The Arcadians had them trapped.

"Magnus Perimeter Command to Transport Night Cutter."

"This is Bishop. Go ahead," Keller replied.

"Your authorization has been granted."

Everyone inside the tiny cockpit breathed a sigh of relief.

"Send your security code and we'll have you on your way."

Alira did as asked, transmitting the sequence Bodan had provided with the vessel. Keller and Alira conversed together, their voices fading into the background as Vernon stared at the lead Arcadian corvette.

"They're not responding," he muttered.

The two Bolarans turned and looked out the viewport. The speakers crackled to life.

"*Transport* Night Cutter, *we've run your security code through our computer and it's coming up as expired.*"

"Bodan..." Keller gritted his teeth. "Apologies, Magnus Control, we've been having problems with our systems. If you'll just give me a moment, I'll ensure the proper code is sent."

Alira muted the channel and pulled out a cable from her pocket. She hooked it up to the computer and plugged the other end into Keller's neck port.

"Now what are you doing?" Vernon asked.

"The scopes of that corvette are doing a deep dive on our systems as we speak to see if we were telling the truth." Alira ran her hands over her console. "Keller's going to take that opportunity to create a connection between the ship's two computers and find a code we can use."

"He's going to piggy back on an Arcadian link and hack into their system?" Vernon directed his attention to the Bolaran leader. "Can you do that without them knowing?"

Keller took a deep breath and closed his eyes. "There's a first time for everything."

Vernon's stomach churned. Behind him, Keller winced, and his eyelids fluttered.

"The connection's been established." Thousands of lines of data scrolled down Alira's monitor. "So far, so good. He's broken through their firewall, now it's just a matter of getting into the mainframe."

Vernon shook his head. He'd seen some crazy stuff in his long life, but what was taking place before him was bordering on the ridiculous. His console beeped, and he checked his scopes. "We've got more company coming our way. The patrol near the fourth moon has altered course."

"He's in the mainframe," Alira said.

More code scrolled down her screen along with a series of graphical displays. He shifted between menus so quickly it blurred together as one. On the scopes, the Arcadian fighters moved into a battle-ready formation, and the corvettes to their port and starboard closed in.

"They're getting suspicious," Vernon told them.

Keller's body started to convulse, and Alira dashed out of her seat to stop him from falling to the deck. "Come on, Keller."

"This is going to kill him."

"We'll all be dead if he can't get this done," she snapped.

"Transport Night Cutter, *we've scanned your systems and—"*

As quickly as the transmission from the leader corvette began, it paused. Silence returned to the channel, and Vernon and Alira stared at each other. Keller stopped trembling, and his eyes burst open. Before either of them could ask him if he was okay, the transmission resumed.

"Transport Night Cutter, *your security code has been cleared,"* the voice filtered over the comms. *"You may continue on to Magnus III."*

Vernon, not needing to be told twice, got them underway, swerving past the lead Arcadian corvette which pushed away, giving them a clear path to the planet. Alira put the exhausted Keller in his seat and let him get some rest. Seconds later, his eyelids closed over.

TWENTY-SEVEN

"I want security at all the airlocks!"

The bridge of the *Defender* turned into a cacophony of noise with orders being yelled back and forth between the officers.

"We have teams making their way to decks three and four!"

"Open up the weapon locker!"

"Thruster control requests fire team assistance!"

"Can we get some power to the maneuvering thrusters?"

Before Logan knew it, a sidearm was being placed in his hand, and the emergency shutter was being brought down over the bridge's rear entry.

"Where are we on those jumpships?" Pollock asked Georgiou.

"I'm picking up seven heading our way," the ensign replied. "They're proceeding to airlocks on both port and starboard sections."

"Coordinate with security and send the bulk of our teams to those locations."

"Aye, sir."

All the voices around Logan overlapped with one another as preparations were made to take on the Arcadian boarding parties. He thought about everything that'd happened since he'd been briefed on the mission to the Corvair Star System. The Arcadian prisoner, the information leading them to the fifth planet, and what steps they'd taken to protect themselves making their way to Artemis Unit's alleged new base of operations. A clunk reverberated throughout the hull, distracting him from piecing it all together.

"That's the first of the jumpships locking on," Georgiou informed Pollock. Moments later, the rest of the smaller vessels filled with Arcadian troops latched on. "One's connecting to deck two on the port side."

Logan went over to Emovic, who'd remained at the combat station. The officer at the controls brought up the interior cameras of the corridor where the security team was preparing for the boarding party. They all waited inside maintenance junctions and wherever else they could find to protect them.

The airlock opened.

A grenade rolled from out of it, and deck two filled with billowing black gas, blinding all the cameras. Gunfire boomed, and men howled in pain. Logan glanced at Novikova, who hadn't moved from Reimer's side.

I can't let this end here.

Another boom sounded on the other side of the video feed, and the smoke cleared. All that remained were a smattering of ORC infantrymen sprawled on the deck with Arcadian soldiers prowling away from the bloodbath.

"Sir, our team on deck two's been overwhelmed," Emovic said to Pollock. "The Arcadians appear to be making their way up to deck one."

"I'm getting similar reports throughout the ship," the

communications officer added. "All primary sections are coming under attack."

Pollock walked over to combat and joined Emovic and Logan, checking the cameras. The team of Arcadians shuffled like panthers down the corridor and toward the opposite side of the shutter protecting the bridge.

Logan pointed at the monitor. "They're planting explosives."

"Stand back!" Emovic directed traffic, getting everyone to safety and the security personnel into the best position to take a shot.

The ORC officers locked down their stations and used their chairs as cover. On the monitor, an Arcadian soldier set the charge and hurried back around the nearest corner.

"Here it comes," Pollock said. "Everyone get ready!"

The two command officers bobbed down and pointed their guns at the door. Logan rushed toward Novikova, pulling her behind the helm console.

They didn't have to wait for long.

The door exploded, and shrapnel burst into the air. Logan snuck a peek from cover, expecting a smoke grenade to roll onto the bridge. But the Arcadians didn't throw one. He furrowed his brow and tried to add up the boarding party's strategy.

A clatter of gunfire sounded, and the Arcadians streamed through, turning the *Defender's* command center into a shooting gallery. Logan put one hand on Novikova's head to keep her from getting struck by a stray bullet and the other on his sidearm, taking potshots at the incoming soldiers. Several fell from the resistance of the *Defender's* bridge crew, but holding the line proved difficult. Georgiou dropped from a barrage of shots to the chest, and his howl echoed around the command center.

"There's too many of them," Logan muttered.

The Arcadians neared, and they made a rush for Pollock. Commander Emovic and the combat officer came out from their cover and took the fight to them.

One Arcadian went down, followed by another. Logan gave them some covering fire, taking out more of the soldiers lunging toward them. He glanced around with the net quickly tightening and spotted an emergency hatch in front of the helm. He grabbed Reimer, who was kneeling beside Novikova. "Where does that lead?"

"The maintenance shaft," the lieutenant said.

"Take her with you."

"Where, sir?"

"Get her to an escape pod."

Novikova shook her head. "I'm not leaving without you."

"I'll be right behind you," Logan promised. "Go, Lieutenant. I'll cover you."

Reimer tugged at Novikova's uniform, and she finally relented. He opened the hatch, and they climbed down the rungs of the ladder.

Emovic fell from a knife wound to his chest, and the combat officer followed with a slash across his throat. Pollock fired a spray from his rifle, but none of the shots made contact. A volley of gunfire came his way and shredded him to pieces. His lifeless form dropped to the deck in a pool of his own blood.

Logan surveyed the bridge from behind the helm console, finding himself the only member of the crew remaining. The Arcadians neared like a pack of zombies, aiming their rifles at him. He checked his escape route and, as hoped, Reimer had left the hatch open for him.

He dove down it, pulling the hatch shut on top of his head.

"Where are we?"

Novikova looked around one corner and then the other. A grenade had gone off, leaving shrapnel over the deck and coolant leaking from the conduits behind the bulkhead. Reimer stopped next to her, sweeping his gun ahead of them.

"This is section seven," he said. "We have to keep going to reach an escape pod."

The pair continued on, wary of their surroundings. Apart from a few of their fallen comrades dead in their path, they were all alone. Around them, the hull shuddered from the firefights still taking place throughout the ship. Novikova wondered how many of the crew were left and if Logan had somehow survived.

Reimer stopped at a junction and checked around the corner. A clattering of gunfire burst in the distance, and he quickly pulled himself back to safety.

"How many of them?" Novikova asked.

"Too many," he said. "They're blocking our path."

"Can we take another route?"

The cogs in the lieutenant's mind cranked. "We can go down a deck and take the aft elevator. But there's no guarantee we won't come up against more Arcadians."

"We should turn back and find Logan," Novikova suggested, pointing the way they'd come.

"He couldn't have survived up there."

His blunt statement hit her like a ton of bricks. From the day she'd stepped foot on the *Defender,* she'd played the good soldier. She never spoke out of turn, always followed her orders, and did everything Reimer asked of her. At that moment, however, she didn't care about the rank pin of the young officer's collar. "He's alive. I know it. So, you can either come with me or stay here."

Her forthrightness caught him off guard, and he peered around the corner again, getting the same reception as before. "Well, I guess we could do it your way."

They went back down the corridor, stopping near the section filled with coolant. Beyond the darkness, a figure emerged at the far end.

"Logan?" Novikova whispered.

Another figure appeared beside him.

Then another.

All were armed with Arcadian standard-issue rifles.

The echo of the *Defender's* crew being slaughtered bounced around Logan as he tiptoed down the corridor. In all his time as James Sutter, he couldn't remember being involved in an operation as deliberate. Rarely were the Empire known for their surgical precision, instead preferring to bludgeon their way to victory.

Gunfire sounded ahead, and he approached the next corner, keeping himself protected from what lay on the other side. Three Arcadians fired their rifles in the opposite direction beyond. Logan couldn't be sure who was the target, but for some reason he knew it was Novikova.

He grasped his gun and took aim at the soldier in the center. With a squeeze of the trigger, he fired and nailed the grunt square in the back.

His two friends retreated to safety, but not before Logan could fire again, taking out the one on the left. The remaining soldier quickly concealed himself inside a maintenance junction and returned serve, forcing Logan back around the corner.

There was another shot.

But it didn't come Logan's way.

He bobbed his head out to find the third soldier sprawled on the deck with a bullet between his shoulder blades.

"Jana?" Logan hurried down the corridor and turned to Novikova kneeling over Reimer's body. The helmsman had hits to his chest and stomach.

"He's dead," she said, almost robotically.

Logan reached for her arm and pulled her to her feet. "Jana..."

"He was just a kid."

Logan so desperately wished to wrap his arms around her. He hoped there'd be time for that later. He checked their route and pressed on to the escape pod. There, with one foot inside was an ORC infantryman.

Novikova seemed to recognize him.

"What's your name?" Logan asked.

He appeared stunned for a second. "Uh, Pitts, sir."

"How many seats are in that pod?"

"Three, sir. I've got two spare."

"Help her inside."

Pitts took her arm, and he assisted her entry inside the tiny lifeboat.

From either direction of the long corridor, the sound of boots pushed toward them. The echo of the soldiers' death march took him back to his days at the academy. Back to the days as a servant of the Empire.

At one end beyond the soldiers, a man appeared.

"Uh-oh."

"What is it?" Novikova asked, strapping herself in alongside Pitts.

"It's—"

"Sutter!" the voice called out from the darkness.

Logan widened his eyes at the booming tone. "It all makes sense now."

Novikova clutched his arm. "Who is it?"

The unmistakable figure stepped into the light. One he hoped he'd never have to see again.

"It's Admiral Jones..." Logan stared deep into Novikova's eyes and squeezed her hand. "You have to go now."

"What!" She unbuckled herself and reached out from the escape pod.

Logan threw her straight back in and slammed the panel next to the door. The airlock closed and hissed, ensuring her and Pitts remained inside. Through the small port, Novikova banged her fist against it, her words unable to be heard. He pressed the next button, and the escape pod launched into the abyss. Hopefully as far away from the *Defender* as it could go.

Two soldiers hurried to Logan's side and took him by his arms, forcing him hard on the deck. Back into the custody of Jones. Back as a prisoner of the Empire.

TWENTY-EIGHT

Corvair V had breathable air, unfortunately, the cold was
so unbearable that if you walked on its surface, you'd instantly be turned into a popsicle. The ceiling of the subterranean flight deck opened, allowing the *Night Cutter* to
slip through below the icy ground. Vernon extended the
ship's landing struts and brought them down.

Not wasting any time, he went with Alira and Keller
to the airlock and followed them down the ramp with the
other Bolaran soldiers. There was a loneliness in their surroundings, even if the environmental systems kept the underground warm enough that he wouldn't have to wear
more than one jacket.

Alira hooked up her device to the panel next to the
interior door. It seemed to take an eternity for the software
to work its way through the Arcadian computer. Just as
Briggs was preparing to rig up some explosives, the door
clicked and unlatched. Alira pushed it open, and the
armed grunts took point.

The passageway on the other side was carved out of
the planet's underground. Even with the warmth, Vernon
couldn't help but feel the chill of the surface raise the hairs
on the back of his neck.

"What do you figure the purpose of this passageway is?" Briggs asked, keeping his rifle pointed ahead of the group.

"I think the bigger question is, what's the emperor doing on a planet like this?" Alira pondered. "Who'd want to spend their twilight years buried on this rock?"

"You said it right there," Keller chimed in. "He's old. If he's been near death for so long, what better place to keep that information away from prying eyes? With the technology the Empire has at their disposal, there might be a vast medical facility beyond the next door keeping him alive."

A ripple of energy appeared in front of them, and a translucent barrier blocked their path halfway down the tunnel. Briggs, being the typical grunt that he was, put his hand on it and pushed it through.

"This isn't so bad." He attempted to pull his hand back, but it wouldn't let go of him. "What the hell?"

One of his soldiers grabbed his arm and tried to yank him free. He had no such luck. An alarm wailed around them, and what little light there was in the passageway dimmed.

"I think we've just figured out what this tunnel's for." Vernon pointed to a computer terminal built into the rock next to the barrier. "Another security system."

Alira rushed to the port and hooked up her device. "It must be reading his DNA and knows were not supposed to be here."

"It's tightening around my wrist," Briggs said through gritted teeth.

Vernon stepped closer to him to find the almost liquid-like translucence compressing the appendage. "He's going to lose that hand if we can't take down this barrier."

"This should've been you, old man! You're dying anyway."

"Just because I'm dying, doesn't mean I'm stupid. Maybe next time you shouldn't stick your hand where it's not meant to be."

Alira slammed down on her keypad. "I can't do it. The computer's processing power's too quick for me."

Everyone turned to the fatigued Keller who lumbered to her side. Alira snatched her device away and linked the Bolaran leader with the Arcadian computer. Briggs howled in agony as the barrier pressed against his skin. Keller's eyes closed, and his eyelids fluttered.

Vernon looked up and down at the strange translucence and deliberated. Against all his better judgment, he put his own arm in the field, and an immediate tension pressed on his skin.

Everyone stared at him with their mouths agape.

Especially Briggs. "Why did you do that?"

"Has the tightness around your wrist lessened?" Vernon asked.

The grunt wiggled his fingers. "A little."

"When there's more than one point of entry, it must need to use more power."

Alira checked the two men's arms, being careful not to touch the barrier. "How did you know that'd work?"

"I didn't." Vernon winced. "It won't stop either of us losing our hands if it's not deactivated, though. I can already feel the pressure increasing."

"You didn't answer my question," Briggs snapped. "Why did you do it?"

"Must be because I'm an old softy."

Keller's body convulsed, much like it had earlier. Alira and one of the soldiers held him upright. Both Briggs' and Vernon's arms started to bleed, as if they were being sliced with a knife. Their cries of pain bellowed out in unison. Vernon swore he could feel it reaching the bone.

"I can't do this anymore!" he yelled, a wooziness taking hold and his vision blurring. He closed his eyes and fell to his knees.

Then it happened.

He reopened his eyes, expecting to discover his hand on the other side of the barrier.

But the barrier was gone.

And his hand was still attached to his arm.

He turned to Keller being unplugged and Alira sitting him down to rest. Vernon grabbed his wrist to find an almost perfect ring of blood around his arm, the cut stinging like hell.

An enormous shadow appeared over him, and he looked up at Briggs, who offered him his uninjured hand. Vernon took it and allowed himself to be hauled up.

"Thanks, old man," the grunt said.

The two men's arms were wrapped in bandages by the medics, and once Keller could walk again without falling over, they continued through the tunnel to the next door. Alira hacked it open, and the group made their way through. The rocky confines of the passageway disappeared and were replaced with the inside of the underground facility.

Vernon expected to be greeted by some resistance. There was no emperor's guard or a security detail of any kind. He followed the rest of the team through the subterranean structure warily. It was modern and clean. He wondered if Keller was right about it being a medical facility.

They marched on through the corridors until they reached the most central location. The room was circular, and surrounding them on the walls were large monitors and workstations beneath each one. Some screens were blank, but others had complicated code scrolling down them.

"This is more like the bridge of a ship. Not an emperor's palace," Briggs said.

Alira went over to the nearest console to access it with Keller and Vernon in tow. "This is incredibly complex." More data scrawled in front of her, and a menu popped up. "Huh?"

"What is it?" Vernon asked.

She pressed in another button and turned.

In the middle of the vast room, a holographic projection materialized. The soldiers stood back from it and gazed at it in stunned silence. Vernon walked up to the holographic figure and rounded it.

"It's the emperor..." Vernon stared at Alira and then at the technology surrounding him. "No sleeping quarters? No kitchen or bathroom facilities?"

"Where's the real emperor?" Briggs asked.

Vernon put his hand through the projection, and it shimmered around him. "I think this *is* the real emperor."

TWENTY-NINE

Fox zipped up his jacket and warmed his coffee on the heating element sitting on his desk. He seemed to feel the cold that little bit more lately. It probably had something to do with all the weight he'd lost since the start of the war. He'd never been a big man, but he'd never had an issue keeping himself healthy. Stress was likely the major factor. As head of the Outer Rim Coalition's leadership, every decision fell to his judgment. Every action taken came down to his choices. Every person who died, did so because of him.

Fox took a sip of his drink, remembering the innocent victims at Gelbrana Colony. He'd found the first reports from the farming world difficult to read. So far, the casualties of the war had been mostly confined to the military personnel of both belligerents. The Empire, nevertheless, had decided to alter its strategy. In the sleepless nights since, he wondered if it was a sign of their desperation, or a message to Bolar and Thandeea, to ensure they didn't become too much of a concern.

Fox placed his mug down and shook his head. Like with everything, he was probably overthinking it. The ORC rebellion had been successful, at least for a time, because of its high level of morale. And while the Empire might've been pressing farther into the Rim, there was still some hope left in those under his command. The massacre of Gelbrana had been a major dent to that morale. Even in the corridors of the leadership, there seemed to be an inevitability in the air that everything was soon at an end.

His door chime sounded, and he looked up from his desk. He pressed the panel at his fingertips, and the door slid open. Hauser walked from the bright corridor and entered the dimly lit office Fox had resided in for the past few weeks.

"You come bearing bad news," he said, noticing the woman's obvious body language.

"You could say that." She pulled out the chair opposite him and slid her data pad across the desk. "You wanted to be informed about the *Defender's* recon mission in the Corvair Star System."

He checked the report. Everyone who served under Fox in the ORC were in his thoughts, but ever since the massacre at the Olarus Nebula, the former Arcadian pilot, who'd been transformed from James Sutter into a hero of the rebellion, always seemed to linger on his mind that little bit more. Sending Nathan Logan to Corvair was a risky move but one that felt right considering his experience with Artemis Unit.

"We had another ship nearby," Hauser continued. "The *Trailblazer's* long-range scopes found debris. Remnants which could've only been of the *Defender*."

"So, no Artemis?"

"It would appear not. The *Trailblazer* picked up an Arcadian carrier moving away from the system on the edge of their range. If I had to take an educated guess, I'd say the *Defender* was ambushed."

"A trap? Why would they bother for one ship? Unless..."

He caught Hauser's gaze. Her frown told him she was thinking along the same lines. "The Empire are canny."

"Unfortunately so." He felt horrible pushing the subject aside, but the war could wait for no single person. Especially not anymore. "What about Vernon? Has he contacted us since leaving Garvin IX?"

"Nothing," she said. "He was last heading toward the core worlds of the Empire."

Into the lion's den.

When first hearing about the mission to assassinate the emperor, Fox had been skeptical, but there was a determination in Vernon's voice he hadn't heard for a very long time. Not since he'd left his allegiance to the Empire behind, deciding to help bring independence to the Outer Rim. From the moment he'd met the man decades earlier, he could see what a skillful pilot he was, along with being an astute tactician and an accomplished teacher. Fox had come across several men and women with similar traits, but Vernon was different. He was a calm soul who'd always had a fire burning beneath the surface. Fox wondered whether working with the Bolarans had stoked that fire. He could only hope his old friend used the burn inside him to do what he sought to do, because the rebellion was fast running out of options.

"Tell the *Trailblazer* to enter the Corvair Star System if safe to do so and look for survivors. Inform me if anything changes," Fox instructed her.

Hauser nodded.

"Is there something else?"

She said nothing at first, instead pursing her lips. "A report's come in from The Jengas Cluster."

"The second fleet?"

She bowed her head. "Wiped out."

"Survivors?"

"None."

Fox stood and walked to the viewport, staring out at the stars beyond his office. "That's thirty-five ships. Over forty thousand personnel."

"They came up against a pincer movement from two Arcadian fleets. From what we understand, the second fleet put up a good fight and took out significant enemy numbers. Ultimately, however, they failed to hold the line."

Fox closed his eyes. He was quickly running out of soldiers. And friends. "Have we got reinforcements in the area?"

"No, our closest reinforcements are in the Klarinda Star System."

"Then the Empire's push toward the Outer Rim's core worlds is speeding up quicker than we expected." He turned and paced behind his desk. "We'll have to start pulling back to consolidate our forces."

"We've been pulling back for months now," Hauser said, her fiery side rearing its head. "Are we just going to keep running?"

"At the moment, we're being picked off one by one. We have to get out of open space and use what numbers we have left to combine into a fighting force able to defend our home."

"You realize we're delaying the inevitable?" Hauser's voice softened. "We could be defeated within a matter of weeks now. Days even."

"No one knows that more than me." Fox handed her the data pad. "It's time we got our hands dirty. There's no need for us to work from the shadows anymore. One extra ship might not make a difference, but if we're going to go down, we'll at least do it with the people we dragged into this godforsaken war. Have the helm set a course out of here."

Hauser rushed out of the office, and Fox returned to his seat.

It won't be long now...

THIRTY

"This won't work."

Alira rubbed her face and stared at the holographic chamber's main console. Keller went to her side, while the rest of the party, including Vernon, remained at the center of the room, next to the eerily accurate representation of the emperor.

"What do you mean?" Keller asked.

"This system's more complex than I thought," she said. "I've come across some pretty impressive software in my time. This—"

"You're going to need me, aren't you?"

Alira looked away from him and tried to access the Arcadian system again. Keller had met few people with the skills she had with a computer. The woman seemed to understand its coding more than the Bolaran language.

Even with all the pain pulsating through his body and the unbearable headaches hammering inside his skull, he could still remember the moment she'd come to him with the idea of fusing man and machine as one. It was a wild notion. At first, Keller had thought she was joking. The more she'd filled him in on her theory, the more convinced he was it might work.

Bolar's rebellion, though dysfunctional at times, did have a knack for bringing together the best their world had to offer. Everyone hated the Empire, apart from the most traitorous of collaborators, so when the brightest minds worked as one, there was nothing they couldn't achieve. When it came to deciding who to fuse the new technology with, there was only one option. Keller had sent more men and women to their death than he could count. He refused to ask anyone else to volunteer for something so ungodly. It had to be him and him alone.

His transformation had changed him both inside and out. When he'd awakened from his surgery on Bolar, the Keller of old still existed, but his experiences and memories no longer flowed through him like they would for anyone else. It was as if they were sitting in a file ready to be downloaded should the need arise. The part that was the old, and the new, fought with each other like a tug-of-war. He'd read about what Artemis Unit had done to Nathan Logan and wondered if he was experiencing a similar battle of wills. He wished he'd asked him before he'd gone back to the Rim.

Luckily for Keller, there was a way to manage the pain. And that was to merge with another computer and do what he was built to do.

It was like a drug.

One that was slowly killing him.

He reached out and grasped Alira's hand. She turned, revealing a deep pit of fear on her soft but powerful features. She hadn't looked at him the same since his surgery. Perhaps she regretted helping create the freak in front of her, or maybe she was just downright frightened of what he'd become.

"We have to do this," he said to her. "We have to understand what's going on here."

Alira relented and pulled the cable from her jacket. "The more we do this, the more—"

"I know." Keller did his best to smile. It only seemed to distress her more.

She plugged the cable into the terminal of the computer and the other in the port in his neck. An immediate jolt of energy zapped down his spine and up again into his brain. He still wasn't used to the sensation, but there was no doubting its addictive properties. A giddiness filled his head, and a numbness surged through his arms and legs.

Keller closed his eyes, and darkness fell over him. The outside world disappeared, and the sound of the computers buzzing and beeping around him faded into obscurity. He blinked his eyelids open again to find himself engulfed in white.

It was like in all the tales he'd been told about the afterlife. In the distance, a black dot appeared. The first time he'd gone through the experience, he'd thought he was dead and that it was a gateway to the next life. As he'd walked toward the dot, he'd quickly discovered it was a transfer point, just not to the paradise promised to him by his childhood priests.

The black dot increased in size with every step he took, becoming something akin to a black hole. Tendrils of energy throbbed from its opening, and when he looked inside, pure nothingness peered back at him.

Keller knew the drill by now and put his hand in front of it. The force of the hole clutched hold of him and yanked him in. His white surroundings disappeared, and a bottomless nightfall rained over him, launching him head-first through oblivion. He spun so fast he wanted to vomit, but nothing came up from his churning stomach. He wondered if it was even possible to throw one's guts up as an avatar inside a computer.

Before Keller could think too much about it, the hole spat him out the other side and sent him sprawling to a floor. The black subsided into a gray and changed into a vivid blue. He covered his eyes for a moment to get used to the brightness surrounding him and dragged himself to his feet. The blue started to spin around him. Slow at first, then faster, as if he were inside a washing machine. A haze of whiteness emerged, and a series of numbers materialized in enormous text.

The feeling of wanting to throw up returned. It quickly subsided with all the numbers becoming clearer. He put out his hands and plucked them from the air. One after another, lining them up before him in a row.

Ten numbers.

One hundred numbers.

One thousand numbers.

They kept coming. Faster and faster.

Then a wave of blue lifted him, tossing him about like a tiny wooden boat in some faraway ocean.

Soon the harsh ripples faded away, and he was back on his feet again. Everything around him was now green, not unlike a forest. However, instead of being surrounded by trees, strange shoots of energy buzzed past him in every direction. The shoots got closer and closer to him with each second until they completely covered him. His vision filled with the neon color, and it turned into pictures and sound. The images and voices moved so rapidly they blended together, producing the records he'd come for.

He could, of course, translate them into something that was recognizable. And when he did, everything became clear.

Is that possible?

How could they have concealed this?

A bright whiteness flashed, and darkness again surrounded him.

"Keller!" a voice spoke inside his mind.

He slowly opened his eyes to find himself back in the holographic chamber, with Alira and Vernon looking over him. "You pulled the connection?" he muttered, realizing he'd been returned to Magnus III.

"Your convulsions," she said. "They were worse this time. Are you okay?"

Keller touched his physical body and pulled himself upright. "I'm still here."

"Well?" Alira asked. "What did you find?"

"You won't believe it..."

THIRTY-ONE

Jana?

Logan walked around the dark brig, feeling his way with his outstretched arms. It hadn't taken long to be subdued by the Arcadian boarding party on the *Defender*. Once he knew Novikova had fled in the escape pod, it wasn't worth putting up much more of a fight.

He could only hope they hadn't captured her.

On his arrival aboard the *Imperator*, he was immediately thrown into the brig. No one uttered a word to him. Not even Jones, who joined him on the trek to the enormous Arcadian carrier. The man's dispiriting eyes, instead, simply bored through him.

The high-ranking officer considered Sutter to be like a son. Logan could only imagine what he'd gone through with everything that'd happened since Sutter had left Artemis Unit on his mission to the Outer Rim. The part of him that was Sutter pitied him. The part that was Nathan Logan couldn't help but think he'd brought it on himself.

Karma's a bitch.

He so desperately wanted to know if Jana was safe. If she was captured, he could only imagine what the Arcadians would do to her.

There was a clunk at the front of the brig, and a slither of light grew from the crack of the door opening. Logan rushed toward it, but a soldier, quick to action, shoved him backward and slammed him into the rear bulkhead.

Logan covered his eyes to shield them from the brightness, and the guard grasped him by his collar, dragging him from his cell. He put restraints around his wrists and pushed him through the detention block. With a nudge, two terse soldiers directed him out into the corridor.

"Where are you taking me?" Logan asked them.

They didn't reply.

He checked his surroundings, seeing if there was any route of escape. He quickly shook his head. It was as if he had to remind himself he was aboard one of the most powerful vessels in all the Empire.

They rounded a corner and hopped inside an elevator. A guard activated the controls, and the car fired up the shaft. It moved so rapidly, Logan thought he'd left his stomach behind. When they arrived, it became obvious where he was heading. In his heart of hearts, he always knew he'd end up there again.

The trio passed several Arcadian officers who looked at him with expressions ranging from disgust to disdain. His story was likely well-known throughout the Empire by now. Eventually, they made their way through the gauntlet and arrived at a door. One of the soldiers pressed the door chime, and a booming voice sounded from the other side.

"Come!"

The doors parted, and the guards ushered him through. The office was filled with a harsh dim light.

It must be the evening on Dylaria.

If it wasn't for his attuned eyes, he likely wouldn't have seen the desk in front of the viewport. A chair behind it faced the other way, while plumes of cigar smoke billowed above it.

"That'll be all," the man sitting in the seat instructed them.

The soldiers looked at each other uneasily and scurried out of the office, closing the door behind them.

In the viewport's reflection, Admiral Jones' eyes, the very same ones that wouldn't stop staring at Logan aboard the jumpship, remained fixed on him.

"Welcome back, James," he said in his raspy tone.

"Welcome back?" Logan said incredulously. "You call this a welcome?"

Jones slowly swiveled in his chair to face him. He placed his cigar in his mouth and took a few more puffs. "I gather you didn't expect to see me again."

Logan had no choice but to take in the fumes of the rancid stogie, unable to wave it away with his hands in their restraints. "I suppose in our business, it's best one never says never."

"True." The admiral put his cigar in the ashtray on his desk. "I hope my men haven't treated you too poorly."

"No. I didn't expect them to. At least not yet. You obviously have other plans for me."

Jones raised his eyebrows. "I'd wondered if you might've figured it out."

"I just wish I'd discovered what your intentions were earlier. It would've saved the *Defender's* crew from getting caught up in all of this." Logan edged closer to the desk. "There was never a new Artemis Unit facility in the Corvair Star System, was there? You planted the information on your pilot, with the intention of her being captured, knowing she'd be interrogated. As far as she knew, that base existed, but really it was all a ruse. You pulled the same trick with her that you did with me on

Brindara, making it appear her craft had been destroyed."

The admiral picked up his cigar and twirled it around in his fingers.

"It was me you wanted all along. And you made a calculated gamble I'd be sent on the mission to find the new base."

"Your powers of deduction are as I remembered," Jones said. "You really were too smart for a flyboy."

"I know you well." Logan shrugged. "Besides, when I left Dylaria, there was that side of me that's still James Sutter that knew you needed to finish the job. The question is, how are you going to do it? Executing a hero of the Empire, no matter my transformation, won't be popular when it gets out. And you know it will. The *Imperator's* a big ship."

Jones sprinkled the ash from his stogie in the ashtray, and an uncharacteristic smile appeared on his weathered face. "Who said anything about killing you?"

Logan craned his neck.

"Artemis Unit may not have a new facility in the Corvair Star System, but they have reopened for business. You'd be aware of that from the hundreds of pilots flying out there, bearing the memory of who was once James Sutter," the admiral told him. "When you returned to us from the Rim as Nathan Logan, we were obviously disappointed with what you'd become. At the time, we hoped your rehabilitation would right that. It was the only chance we had of seeing the old Red Hawk again. There was no way we could risk wiping your mind a second time."

A lump formed in Logan's throat. "You're saying something's changed?"

"With Artemis under new management, those in

charge now believe we can wipe what's up there for a second time without doing any discernable damage."

"You plan to do to me what you've done to those pilots."

"That's correct, James. The memory engrams given to them are those of James Sutter before he traveled to the Rim. When those engrams are implanted, the old James Sutter will return to the body standing before me. It'll be as if you hadn't even left." Jones pulled out a pair of unsmoked cigars from his pocket with distinct red rings around them, indicating they were Jontorian Specials. "You're right, however. An execution will take place. Soon, the mind of Nathan Logan will no longer exist. Once the surgery's done with, we can smoke these in celebration as admiral and captain once again."

THIRTY-TWO

Alira and Briggs helped Keller onto the floor, propping him up against the wall and keeping him as upright as possible. The Bolaran medic kneeled by his side and waved his medical probe over him.

"How is he?" Alira asked.

The medic checked the readings. "He's—"

"It doesn't matter right now," Keller said.

"It does matter!" Alira snapped. "The more we keep doing—"

"I knew the risks before we started this back on Bolar. *All* of us knew the risks." Keller dragged himself up, and Vernon and the others moved out of his way, giving the Bolaran leader some space.

Keller grasped at his head and wobbled uneasily on his feet. He blinked a few times and stumbled toward the hologram in the middle of the chamber. Vernon and Alira followed him and stopped in front of the emperor's projection.

"What did you find in there?" Vernon asked.

"Where would you like me to begin?" he said.

Alira edged closer to him, taking his arm, probably fearing that at any moment he might collapse to the floor.

"It's definitely no medical facility." Keller gestured to their surroundings. "It's not some underground palace either. It was constructed ten years ago, around the time it's believed the emperor left Arcadia."

"But he's not here."

"No, he's not. In fact, he never came here."

Briggs joined the trio along with the rest of his soldiers, just as keen to see what Keller had discovered on his journey inside the facility's computer.

"Ten years ago, the emperor died in his bed," the Bolaran leader revealed.

Silence filled the chamber, and for some strange reason, Vernon looked at the emperor's hologram. It wasn't just a projection but a ghost of the man who once was.

"What happened to him?" Alira asked.

"Ironically, it would seem he was taken by old age. Of all the assassination attempts, the pressure of keeping the Empire together, and overseeing the deaths of millions, it was finally Father Time that finished the job."

"And this place was built, as what, a monument to him?" Briggs said.

Vernon shook his head. Briggs was a good soldier, but his understanding of what they'd found was severely lacking. "How can this be a monument, when everyone throughout the Empire and beyond believe the emperor's still alive?"

"That's right." Keller nodded. "Apart from us, it would appear only one man is aware of the emperor's true fate."

"The one responsible for this place..."

"When he figured the emperor was about to die, he built this facility and transported him off Arcadia. Those in the highest echelon of the Empire thought the emperor was brought here for his own protection. In fact, he died in transit and was shot out of a missile tube just like any run-of-the-mill soldier."

Vernon's mind took him back to the day he'd been wounded during the Bolaran conflict as a young pilot. The day the emperor visited him and the rest of the troops.

The day she died.

"Who did it?" Vernon asked. "You spoke of one man orchestrating this. Who's responsible?"

"A councilor." Keller pushed at his temples. "His name's McCrae."

"McCrae..." Vernon moved away from the group and stopped in front of the main control console. He'd met him the same day as the emperor. If he was like any of the others who sat on the Emperor's Council, he was a very powerful man who'd gained significant wealth throughout his career. "It all makes sense."

Everyone in the holographic chamber turned to him.

"Think about it. What did we talk about before coming here? The whole idea of assassinating the emperor was to fracture the Empire. This is what McCrae feared when the emperor was on his death bed ten years ago. Normally when the leader of the Empire dies, his title falls to his heir. But this emperor had no children, and all of his relatives were killed in the Great Purge. It was decided long ago, the next ruler would be chosen by the council when the day came. It very well could have done exactly what we were trying to achieve, splintering the Empire in two or more parts."

Alira glanced at Vernon and then at Keller. "So, Mc-Crae covered up his death."

"He may not have thought he'd be appointed the emperor's role, so he figured what better way to take power while keeping stability throughout the Empire."

"Exactly," Keller said. "This hologram's projected into

the council chambers back on Arcadia and gives them its instructions not dissimilar to how the emperor would have from his palace. As far as the other councilors are concerned, it's the emperor handing them his orders, when in reality it's a sophisticated computer program controlled by McCrae."

"If that's the case, this is an even better situation than we thought," Briggs said, seeming to finally understand.

"He's right," Vernon told them. "When everyone finds out about the fraud McCrae's orchestrated, all the other councilors will band against him. Civil war's almost a certainty."

"Then we have to get word out." Alira walked toward Vernon at the main console. "It should be just a matter of using this facility's comms network to send a transmission throughout the Empire."

"This can't come from one of us," Keller said. "They won't believe a Bolaran, regardless of the proof we've got." He lurched toward them and stopped next to Vernon. "You were once a hero of the Empire."

"*Once* being the operative word," Vernon countered. "I'm as much an enemy of the state as you."

"There's no other way."

The expectant faces of the Bolarans gazed at him. Suddenly, he wasn't just the old fossil who'd been brought along for the ride. "Very well."

Alira tapped the comms panel and activated a channel. "When you're ready."

He moved in front of the monitor, and a green light indicated the camera was recording. He gathered himself and tried to put the words together. "My name's Charles Vernon, and I'm about to inform you of the greatest lie in the Empire's history—"

Suddenly, all the lights throughout the chamber

winked out, and the monitors deactivated. Even the holo-gram of the emperor shimmered from existence.

Briggs clutched his rifle. "What's happening?"

Alira slammed the console. "It looks like I tripped a safety algorithm when I began the broadcast."

"Which means we have to move!" Keller staggered to-ward the exit. "If we don't leave this place alive, no one will ever know what happened here."

THIRTY-THREE

"We're approaching Corvair V, ma'am."

Captain Waters walked toward the *Trailblazer's* helmsman, crossing her arms behind her. The mesmerizing colors of the gas giants swirled before them. "Any enemy activity on the scopes?"

Off to the port side of the bridge, Lieutenant Steele shook his head. "Not since we spotted the carrier hyperwarping out of the system."

Waters didn't trust the Arcadians. She'd been in countless scraps with them in the past few months and served on the front lines long enough to know what they were capable of. While combat using overwhelming force was their mantra, she couldn't discount their cunning either. And knowing the *Defender* likely met its untimely fate in orbit of Corvair V made her that much warier. "Don't take your eyes off those scopes, Lieutenant. If you see any Arcadian bogeys pop up, send the coordinates to the helm."

"Yes, ma'am," Steele replied.

She put her hand on the back of her helmsman's chair. "And, Ensign Vickers, if they do make a surprise appearance, don't wait for the order. Just get us the hell out of here."

Vickers nodded without taking her eyes from the helm. She skillfully glided the *Trailblazer* into orbit, and ahead a debris field appeared. A lump formed in Water's throat at the destruction dancing on the backdrop of the enormous planet. She'd never met Captain Pollock before but had read of his exploits during the war. The rebellion was losing too many men and women like him. Soon there wouldn't be enough of them left to keep up the fight.

She paced behind Vickers, recalling the rudimentary scan they'd taken when the *Trailblazer* entered the system. At such a distance it was difficult to get a precise reading of what had happened. The scopes were reliable, but they weren't perfect. With what was in front of them, though, there was now no doubt.

"What's the makeup and composition of the field?" Waters asked Steele, strolling over to her.

He didn't reply straight away, checking and double-checking all his readings and using the computer to calculate the size of the debris and the materials it was composed of. "It's confirmed," he said with an audible sigh. "This was definitely the *Defender*."

"Do a thorough scan of the area." Waters frowned. "If there are any survivors here, I want to know about it."

She made her way to the center of the bridge and stopped next to her Executive Officer, Commander Telcourt.

"You know the Empire doesn't leave survivors behind, right?" he told her.

Waters didn't have to be reminded. "We won't hang around here any longer than we have to, but we owe it to the crew of the *Defender* to at least look."

"Understood." Telcourt scratched his chin. "What do you think happened here, Captain?"

Waters was aware her XO wasn't asking such an obvious question. He was much too nuanced for that. A blind man would realize the *Defender* had walked headlong into a trap. His real question was: Why was the trap laid? "There can only be two possibilities. One: The Arcadians figured we'd send more ships, giving them the opportunity to ambush a decent-sized ORC battle group."

"That doesn't make much sense," he said. "For starters, they know how short on manpower we are right now, and even if we wrangled a sizeable force together, the Arcadians only sent a carrier to greet the *Defender*."

"That's why it's likely possibility two: They wanted Nathan Logan." Waters' mind drifted to the pilot. Everyone knew of his victories and his complicated past. If it was Logan they were after, and they got him, she could only fear what they'd do with him.

The wait continued, and she walked around the bridge, visiting her anxious officers at their stations. They were, of course, sitting ducks in the Corvair Star System. But really, the atmosphere wasn't that different from usual. The war effort was going badly, with little in the way of victories for the rebellion. Everyone, without admitting it, knew the Empire was steadily squeezing the life out of what was left of the ORC, and if Gelbrana Colony was any indication, the Arcadians were hell-bent on lighting the Rim on fire for all to see.

"Ma'am?"

Waters snapped out of her daze and went over to Steele at the scopes. "What have you found?"

"Nothing," the lieutenant informed her. "I'm not detecting any survivors in the wreckage."

Waters sighed, unsurprised. "Ensign Vickers, set a

course out of here. Take us back to the Rim. Best possible speed."

"Yes, ma'am," came the acknowledgment from the helm.

Waters returned to the heart of the bridge, and Commander Telcourt gave her a knowing look. The pair said nothing, and the *Trailblazer* pushed away from Corvair V to make a dash for it.

How many more people are going to die?

"Wait a minute, Captain."

Both Waters and Telcourt turned to Steele's deep voice, which completely betrayed his boyish features.

"I'm reading...something."

Waters stepped toward him. "Something?"

"It's... Well, I'm not sure."

"Bring us to a full stop," Waters ordered Vickers. "Can you be more precise, Lieutenant?"

"There was no sign of anything but debris in the wreckage, but when we altered course, I decided to point the scopes at the planet, just for the hell of it."

"And?"

"Listen for yourself." He pressed in a key, and the speakers came to life with a wavy, almost ethereal tone. But it wasn't quite natural. There was an odd, erratic pattern to it.

Waters widened her eyes. "You realize what that is, don't you?"

Telcourt joined her side. "That's a coded ORC distress signal."

"And it's repeating," Steele said. "If I had to guess, I'd say someone is using a comms array inside the planet's atmosphere to bounce their signal through it to make it sound like it was a natural occurrence. If the Arcadians found it, they likely wouldn't be any the wiser."

"Can something survive down there?"

"We're about to find out." Waters squeezed Steele's shoulder. "I'm glad we've got your ears, Lieutenant. Send the coordinates of the signal to the helm. Vickers, take us about."

Ensign Vickers did as instructed and turned *Trailblazer* back in the direction of Corvair V, bringing the great mass into full view. The ship quickly closed in on the violent atmosphere. Waters moved to the viewport and peered out at the deep-blue gases, making it seem as if there were a tempest being unleashed upon the world.

"Lieutenant Indarin," she said to her communications officer. "Direct a message out there that we're an ORC vessel on a rescue mission."

Indarin nodded and ran her hands over the console. "I'm not receiving a reply."

"Scopes?"

"There doesn't appear to be any movement, but the signal is definitely emanating from beneath that atmosphere," Steele replied.

"Keep replaying the message, Lieutenant."

"Yes, ma'am," Indarin said.

"Perhaps we should go fishing," Telcourt suggested from the center of the bridge.

Waters raised her eyebrows. "Would our grapple reach their position?" she asked her man at the scopes.

Lieutenant Steele nodded. "I believe so."

"Then let's throw out a line."

The *Trailblazer's* long grapple cable launched from its ventral housing and burst into Corvair V's atmosphere. Hitting something would be a miracle, but if the survivors saw them, they might hopefully see them as being friendly and maneuver their vessel toward it.

Telcourt passed the helm station and went over to the

captain. "If this doesn't work, would you like me to take a jumpship down there?"

It wasn't an order Waters wanted to give. As she was about to tell him to prepare a ride, Steele interrupted her.

"Ma'am, the grapple's got hold of something!"

The *Trailblazer's* two command officers rushed over to him.

"Reel them in!" Waters ordered.

The long grapple slowly wound back into its housing, and the small craft emerged from the upper layer of the atmosphere.

"An escape pod," Telcourt murmured. "Lieutenant Indarin, is there any comms activity?"

"No," she said. "Still nothing."

"Whoever's in there could be dead for all we know."

Waters ran to the exit. "Have a medical team meet me at the airlock!"

THIRTY-FOUR

"Go! Go! Go!"

Briggs ushered everyone through the last door of the tunnel as it gradually closed from above. Whatever security protocols were in place didn't give them all much time to get out. Vernon sprinted with all the others from the holographic chamber, not wanting the underground facility to become his tomb.

He ran as fast as he could, languishing behind them, unable to keep up with the younger men. Even Keller was quicker than him. Briggs put out his hand, and Vernon took it, allowing the soldier to pull him through the door just before it clanged shut.

Everyone rushed toward the ship, sitting at the heart of the flight deck, and hurried up the ramp. Vernon, almost out of breath, staggered up it, through the rear compartment and into the cockpit. Alira sat Keller down at the station off to the side and activated the communications array.

A few moments passed, and she slammed her fist into the console. "The code the Arcadian patrol provided to open the bay doors doesn't work!"

"They don't want us to leave." Vernon sat at the helm and got the briefest of flight checks out of the way.

"We might have only one choice available to us."

Keller, looking even worse for the journey, didn't utter a sound. He was so out of it from their escape, he likely wasn't even registering where he was.

"Hooking him up to the computer again?" Vernon said. "There might be another way. From memory, this craft has a dorsal missile tube."

Alira's eyes widened at what he was suggesting. "Doing that could very well kill us."

"Would you prefer to be an Arcadian prisoner?" Her lack of answer told him all he needed to know. "Besides, these K2-Class transports were built pretty tough."

Alira didn't look too convinced, but she must have known, like him, Keller was in no state to save the day again. "Do it!"

Briggs appeared behind them from the rear compartment. "What are we doing about that door?"

"We're going to blow a hole in it." Vernon activated the vessel's weapon grid. "I'd suggest you tell everyone in the back to buckle up."

Briggs went to say something but must've thought better of it, quickly leaving the cockpit. Alira wrapped the seat's straps around Keller, while Vernon secured his own. The targeting computer came online, and he armed the single warhead in the dorsal missile tube, aiming it at the center of flight deck door above them.

"You should get in the back and take a seat, too," he told Alira.

"No. If you can't pull this off, we're dead regardless," she said. "If a chunk of that thing falls on us, we'll be crushed like a tin can."

"Your faith in me is very reassuring." The crosshairs

on their target blinked red. "Are you ready?"

She nodded and grabbed hold of Vernon's chair. He gently lifted the ship from the deck and hovered them slightly off center. He double-checked his target and put his finger over the trigger.

He fired.

The missile launched from the dorsal tube.

Without a moment to blink, it exploded into the door.

Vernon avoided the flying debris as the ceiling above their heads rained down on them. A huge chunk broke off and plummeted toward their position, forcing him to get creative and use a combination of maneuvers to avoid it.

A cascade of blasts went off throughout the flight deck, and the ship rocked from the tinier pieces of debris.

"Might be time we got out of here!" Alira yelled over the din.

Vernon pushed in the commands, and they rose from what was quickly turning into a pit of fire. They rode out the orange flames, and the continued tinging of large alloy shrapnel hammered into their armored hull.

The icy surface of Corvair V appeared, and the hellfire left behind them quickly became a memory.

"Is everyone in one piece?" Vernon asked, pushing the vessel farther into orbit.

Alira nodded, and Keller, still far from himself, gave him a wry smile. "We might not have the Red Hawk with us anymore," he said, "but, luckily, we've got the next best thing."

The ship cleared the planet's thin atmosphere, and the proximity alarms wailed. Vernon checked his scopes, discovering bogeys ahead and to starboard. "The Arcadians are heading our way. There won't be any fooling them this time. Once they're in range, they won't be asking any questions. I'm preparing to enter hyperwarp."

He found an empty lane through the incoming vessels and let the navigational computer do the calculations. "Stand by." He activated the hyperwarp drive, but only a faint whine from the engine responded to his command.

"What's going on?" Alira asked.

Vernon checked the automated damage report. "Our hyperwarp's offline. It must've been damaged when we were fleeing the flight deck."

Alira cursed and leaned over Keller at the side workstation. "I'll try to send a transmission back to Bolar. If they can take the proof of what we've found and spread it throughout the Empire, it won't matter if we make it or not."

Vernon readied the maneuvering thrusters to give her the time she required. If he could find even a few extra minutes before they were destroyed, it might be all they needed to turn the war in their favor.

Smaller bogeys, representing enemy missiles, appeared on the scopes.

"They're firing!" Vernon evaded to port, narrowly avoiding the first Arcadian salvo. The second whizzed by, shaking the starboard hull. "Have you sent that message yet?"

Alira punched at the console. "We're being jammed. I can't broadcast anything!"

"Then you should probably get that hyperwarp engine up and running," Keller said to her, still quite woozy. "And you... You can show us that guy from all the stories I heard as a kid. Just remember whose side you're on this time."

Alira didn't hesitate and sprinted out of the door to the engine room. Vernon let the insult slide and focused his attention on the helm. He could never right all the wrongs he'd performed in his lifetime, but he could at least do his damnedest to give those around him their best chance.

THIRTY-FIVE

Logan snapped his eyes open and shielded them from the harsh light beaming above him. He furrowed his brow and slowly removed his hands from his face.

Where the hell am I?

He tried to move but found himself restrained by a harness over his shoulders and waist.

A cockpit?

Logan took his belts off and pulled himself from his seat, unlatching the canopy and letting the outside air rush in. Sand covered the ground, and mountainous rock formations surrounded his craft in all directions.

"Brindara?"

The moment he'd first awakened on the barren moon was etched in his memory. They were, after all, the first moments Nathan Logan had experienced. On that fateful day, he'd known nothing. Not who he was, where he was, or why he'd awakened inside the cockpit of a downed fighter.

So, what am I doing back here?

Logan got out of the cockpit and jumped onto the surface via the starboard wing. The near unbearable heat of the planet beat down on him, and sweat beaded on his forehead. He dabbed it away with the sleeve of his orange flight suit and stepped through the sand toward the nearest wall of rock.

When he turned around to look at his beached fighter, it was gone. No longer was he ankle-deep in soft sand, instead higher up the summit, staring down from above. At the bottom, he spotted his craft. It was little more than a speck so high up. Over the other edge was a wasteland of nothingness, leading all the way to the horizon.

The blue Brindaran sky disappeared and became night. In the distance, a flash of lightning flared against the darkness. More strikes approached his position, along with the booming claps of thunder.

Then the rain came down. Only a few drops at first, but soon, however, it was as if a monsoon had swept over him.

Logan tried to make a dash for it. He slipped and fell. He couldn't get a hold of anything and careened over the edge, flinging his limbs about and yelling at the top of his lungs.

There was a thump, and a sharp pain rippled through his body. He slowly heaved himself up to discover he'd landed on a metallic surface. It wasn't the ground. It was a jumpship. Flipping over, he gazed across at an airlock opening, and a slither of light appearing from inside the vessel.

A figure emerged from the hatch, blocking out the light. Then she appeared, just as she had the first time he'd met her on Brindara. She waved a lock of her dark hair aside, and her kind eyes stared at him. Novikova reached for him, and he put out his hand. But as they were about to touch, she began to dissolve.

Her arms went first. Then her legs and the rest of her

body until all that was left was her smile. That, too, disappeared into a void of nothingness.

"Jana!"

The jumpship vanished molecule by molecule too. And then it was his turn. His legs dissolved, and then his waist. It reached his chest along with his arms. A tingle shot up his neck and neared his head.

"Captain Sutter!"

He blinked his eyes open, and more light greeted him. This time it wasn't from the sun but a brightness from outside his cell aboard the *Imperator*.

He rubbed his face and brushed his hand through his unkempt hair, dragging himself up from his hard bed.

"You've been summoned by the admiral," an armed guard informed him.

Logan pulled himself to his feet. The soldier put restraints around his wrists and moved aside to let him through. Another guard appeared, and the pair flanked him out of the detention block into the outer corridor. They led him on a different path from his last visit, into the rear elevator. The car went down the shaft, all the way to the bottom deck of the vessel where the door slid open, revealing the bowels of the *Imperator*.

The trio set off down the long corridor, while every step they took echoed around them. Logan felt like he was being marched to his execution. As Jones had said, in a way he was.

They reached the next access point, and the guards keyed in their authorization code. The door opened into a much larger space with computers lining the walls and medical equipment as far as the eye could see. Several civilians roamed around in white coats, making the scene very similar to the one James Sutter had encountered when he'd first arrived at Artemis Unit.

The soldiers stopped him from walking any farther with a firm hand on his shoulder. At the center of the laboratory, Admiral Jones conversed with a woman in one of the white coats. He glanced sideways, noticing Logan's arrival. He directed the guards to bring him closer.

"James, I'd like you to meet Doctor Vanstrom. She replaced Agata after you took out our Artemis facility in the Dylaria Star System."

"Was Agata there when we destroyed it?" Logan asked.

"No. We'd evacuated everyone well in advance. His death came later. As far as Artemis was concerned, all of its experiments were shipped to a safe location. And before you ask, yes, it was your friend, Doctor Freeman, who gave us the information you'd be making a run at the facility. My interrogators saw to it that he revealed everything."

"What have you done with him?"

"Executed. There wasn't much left after the trimurilene."

Logan clenched his fists together in his restraints.

"It's a pleasure, Captain Sutter," Vanstrom said. "I never got to meet you when you went through the program at Artemis, but I've been studying your case for some time. Your courage in undertaking the mission to the Outer Rim was quite something."

Logan glowered at her. "Yes, and look where it got me."

"I think you'll be interested in this, James." The admiral gestured to the stasis chamber before them. He yanked the lid ajar, and the sound of the seal breaking hissed from the edges.

Inside it was a woman in an Arcadian fighter corps uniform. Vanstrom gave her an injection, and the pilot's eyes began to open. At first, she was startled, but slowly but surely, appeared to understand her surroundings.

"Admiral?" she said with a raspy throat.

"Captain." Jones gave her a hand, and she took it, pulling herself up and stretching out all her muscles. "James, I'd like you to meet Captain Sutter."

Logan craned his neck at the woman, and she, too, gazed at him curiously.

"Captain Sutter." Jones directed his attention to the female pilot. "Can you tell me what planet you were born on?"

"Dylaria, of course," she replied.

"And your wife's name?"

"Kathy."

"And your children's names?"

"Sean and Aud—"

"Enough! I get your point." Logan peered past them at the ten other stasis chambers being thawed out, filled with other pilots who also thought they were James Sutter.

"Don't hate the admiral for this, Captain," Vanstrom said. "He's proving to you this transfer will be safe. Before long you'll be just like your old self."

"That's what I'm afraid of."

"The doctor here has informed me you'll need to be prepared before your surgery," Jones told him.

"It won't be much," she assured him. "I just need to take some brain scans and give you a few injections to en-sure your neocortex is ready for the procedure."

The admiral eyed the soldiers, and they took Logan by each arm, dragging him to the nearest spare bed.

Kicking and screaming to his execution.

THIRTY-SIX

"Here comes another one!"

Vernon evaded the next missile coming from astern, doing his best to flee the pursuing Arcadian vessels. At the side workstation, Keller slowly recovered from his sprint through the underground facility, keeping a close eye on the scopes and letting Vernon know where and how many enemy bogeys were heading their way.

They'd already taken a few hits but managed to charge away from the patrol ships still in one piece. At least for the moment. More of the Arcadian vessels mobilized and joined their comrades in the chase, massively outgunning the *Night Cutter*. Vernon did what he could do to keep them alive, while in the engine room, Alira tried her best to get the hyperwarp engine online.

"Have you attempted sending out that transmission again?" Vernon asked.

"All outgoing frequencies are being jammed," Keller said. "There's no way they'll let us broadcast anything out of this system."

More missiles fired, and Vernon dragged the craft first to port and then to starboard, narrowly avoiding the incoming salvos. "Engine room!" He slammed down on the comms panel. "Have you got an update down there?"

White noise greeted him across the speakers until finally a clunk sounded and a voice filtered through from the other end. *"Stand by,"* Alira advised.

"Once upon a time, I might've been able to take on a battle group of that size. These days—"

"If anyone else were piloting we'd be already dead," Keller interjected.

"That's probably the nicest thing you've said to me."

"Must be all this hard-wiring," the Bolaran quipped.

More enemy missiles appeared on the scopes, and Vernon prepared to pull every maneuver out of the book he could muster. Then the speakers crackled to life.

"I think I've got the hyperwarp up and running."

Vernon didn't hesitate and calculated a course out of the system. Their best route of escape appeared on his monitor, and he activated the hyperwarp drive.

At first, there was silence. Soon after, the same groan which cried out through the hull from earlier.

The Arcadian missiles continued to soar toward them from opposing angles on a converging course. Vernon used the main thrusters in conjunction with the dorsal thrusters to shoot them up the z-axis to avoid being destroyed. A rush of blood went to his head, and the pair of enemy projectiles collided, obliterating each warhead.

Alira ran through the door into the cockpit and did a double take between the two men. "Why the hell haven't we gone to hyperwarp!"

"It didn't work," Keller said.

"What?"

"It wasn't your fault." Vernon examined the damage report. "All the fuel conduits have been fried. More damage from Corvair V. If you did manage to fix it, we might've blown ourselves up anyway."

Alira reached over Keller and attempted to send the message again. "There's no way we'll get that broadcast out of here."

Vernon said nothing, instead peering ahead where a smattering of small asteroids appeared. They were the universal sign you were about to enter a treacherous region of space and that you should turn back.

"What are you doing?" Alira asked, moving to his side.

He continued headlong into the asteroid field. "Those Arcadian ships are much bigger than the *Night Cutter*. Until they get a carrier out here and send some fighters after us, they'll have to be cautious."

"The Red Hawk's not at the controls this time. Are you sure you can do it without getting us killed?"

"He's got this far," Keller said.

A shock of adrenaline surged through Vernon, and he took them inside the field, weaving around the first of many dangerous asteroids. The Arcadian ships in pursuit slowed.

"You know, even in here, they'll still keep jamming us," Alira told him. "At some point we'll have to figure out a way to get our message out."

"I know," Vernon said. "Luckily, I have an idea."

I feel like I've been hit by an ore hauler!

Novikova opened her eyes to her blurry surroundings. A soft blue light illuminated above her head, and she rolled over, putting her hands on her face to shield herself from the brightness. "Where...where am I?"

Several footsteps sounded around her, and a hand

touched her shoulder. She flinched and returned to her back. A woman and a man stood before her, both adorned in ORC uniforms.

The female moved closer to her. "My name's Captain Waters. You're aboard the ORC corvette, *Trailblazer*. How are you feeling, recruit?"

Novikova wiggled her fingertips and patted down her body. "I, uh, seem to be in one piece."

"How is she, Doctor?" Waters asked the man on the other side of the bed.

"It was lucky we found her when we did. The escape pod's oxygen supply was running extremely low when we rescued her," the doctor said. "She's got a mild case of hypoxia, but she'll be fine with some treatment."

"What about Pitts?"

"The other recruit?" The doctor stepped aside and revealed another bed next to hers, with the unmistakable form of recruit Pitts lying on top of it. A breathing apparatus was affixed over his unconscious face. He was so much more serene than the day he and his friends had been joking around at her expense on the flight deck of the *Liberty Cry*. "He hasn't fared as well as you, but he should be okay with some time. It'll just take him a little longer to get out of the woods."

Novikova thought about everyone else who'd perished aboard the *Defender*.

And Logan...

"What's your name, recruit?" Waters asked her.

She plopped her head back on the pillow. "Novikova."

"Recruit Novikova, what training were you undertaking?"

"Flight operations."

"Were you on the bridge of the *Defender* when it arrived in the Corvair Star System?"

She nodded.

Waters grabbed a chair and put it next to the bed, taking a seat beside her. "What happened?"

Novikova replayed it all in her mind. "We entered the system and slowly closed on the fifth planet. When we got there, we searched for Artemis Unit's new facility. But there wasn't anything there. Not in orbit or anywhere else near the planet. Then the Arcadians came."

"It was a trap?"

She nodded again. "They were waiting for us the entire time. But they didn't destroy the ship. At least not straight away. They disabled us first and boarded."

Waters turned away from her to another man who entered with commander rank pins on his uniform. "They wanted Logan, didn't they?"

Novikova refused to think about it anymore. All she'd done was think about it from the moment her and Pitts had left the *Defender* in their escape pod to find a hiding spot in Corvair V's atmosphere. But there was no doubting it. Everything led to Admiral Jones. "We have to find him, Captain."

"Get some rest. I'll send a communiqué to my superiors and inform them of what we know."

"But—"

Waters put a forceful hand on her shoulder to keep her down. "Sleep, recruit. That's an order."

The doctor injected her with something into the side of her neck. Soon the blurriness resumed, and she drifted back into her slumber.

THIRTY-SEVEN

"Are you sure this will work?"

Vernon examined the scopes, only just barely hearing Alira sitting at the starboard side of the cockpit. "It depends. Do you have a better idea?"

She contemplated for a moment and shook her head. "If you believe this is the best way, I guess my life is in your hands."

"Don't sound so enthusiastic," he said. "If I can't pull off this maneuver, it's pretty much guaranteed we'll be dead. And even if we get over there—"

"You leave that to us. Just don't kill us in the meantime."

A bogey appeared on the edge of the scopes and joined several others which were moving throughout the asteroid field. The Arcadians had coordinated a standard search pattern with the ships available to them and were still yet to send in any fighters. It was relatively slow going, but it wouldn't be that way for long.

"Seems like we've got some company heading in this direction." Vernon refocused the scopes on their position and the incoming Arcadian corvette. He peered out at the asteroid they'd parked on, not long after they'd entered the field. The barren landscape of jagged rock, great valleys, and deep fissures was a sight to behold even if it was devoid of life.

With the *Night Cutter* powered down and all but a few priority systems such as the scopes and the air filtration still online, Vernon hoped they'd be impervious to their enemy's scans. Especially considering the high concentrations of nurium in the meteors. So far, his risk had paid off, however, no Arcadian had been as close as the approaching corvette.

Vernon kept a finger on the main power systems, ready at a moment's notice to get the ship going should their cover be blown. One shot from orbit, and the asteroid would become their tomb.

The corvette moved in and flew directly over their position. "They're certainly being methodical," Alira said, checking the scopes at her station.

"They know they can't afford to let us escape." Vernon didn't take his eyes away from the monitor on the helm. The bogey buzzed around for several moments and gradually departed. "All right, here's our chance."

He took his finger from the main systems and prodded at the thrusters. With a pump, he fired the ventral jets and lifted the landing struts, launching off the asteroid. With another push, he set a course toward the corvette. Ideally, with the nurium interference, they'd appear to be an insignificant meteor. At worst, the Arcadians would spot them on their scopes and see them for what they truly were. If that were the case, the next few seconds would be their last.

The corvette didn't stop, continuing on its course around the asteroid. Vernon used the softest of touches on the ship's jets to place them in the perfect position to establish contact. He even threw them into a tumble, just to make it look like they were a tiny asteroid.

"So far, so good." Vernon rubbed his sweaty hands down his pants legs. "Are they sorted back there?"

Alira got on the intercom and sent a message to the rear compartment. "They're ready."

The corvette went from the size of a marble to that of a grapefruit. Even at such glacial speeds, both ships were traveling infinitesimally quicker than what one would assume if they were watching from the surface of the asteroid.

"It'll take some slowing down," Alira warned him. "Are you sure—"

"I don't need a backseat driver right now." Vernon made a slight course adjustment. "Perhaps you should head out back. I'm sure Keller could use your help."

The Bolaran woman thought about it for a moment and took off her harness. With one last look at him, she bailed through the exit. Vernon pressed a button on his console and closed the door behind her.

The proximity alarm on the scopes wailed as two more Arcadian vessels neared. The trajectory was as close as he was going to get, but he was coming in hot. Too hot.

He pounded on the dorsal maneuvering jets, bringing the ship to equilibrium and slowing its momentum. The space around him disappeared, and the hull of the Arcadian corvette took up his entire view. Knowing the design of the ship as well as he did, he adjusted his heading to the port side and headed for the first airlock he could find.

His velocity was still too fast, so he fired the thrusters one last time, lining them up as best he could. He made contact softly, clunking against the other hull, barely scraping the paint off the two vessels.

I've still got it...

Alira stood well back from the airlock, allowing the soldiers to take their places each side of it. Briggs grabbed the manual override lever and pulled it down, revealing a path between the two ships.

Everyone raised their weapons and pointed them through the heart of the opening. But there wasn't a single Arcadian soldier in sight.

"They mustn't know we're here yet," Briggs said.

Keller heroically took the lead. "They will soon. Let's move."

Briggs ushered the rest of them into the corvette's corridor in a defensive formation. They rounded a corner and found themselves in a section connecting two other passageways.

"We must be on one of the habitat decks." Alira indicated the many doors with nameplates on them. "We've got to find a maintenance junction."

Farther they continued until they reached what they were after. Alira pressed on the panel, and the narrow door slid open, revealing the interior of the junction. She attempted to step inside, but Keller stopped her, taking her place instead. He put out his hand, and she shook her head.

"I'm not hooking you up to this thing," she told him.

"We've got to do this quick," he said. "We both know this is the only way to do that."

Alira glanced around at the soldiers guarding their position and then back at him. She finally relented and revealed the cable from her jacket, attaching it to the ports in his neck and the Arcadian computer.

Keller winced and closed his eyes. At that moment, Alira wondered if it was all worth it. Her selfishness took over, and she wished she'd never come up with the idea of merging him with the technology surgically implanted inside him. Every time he was hooked up to another computer, a little part of him disappeared.

Soon there'll be nothing left.

Then reality hit Alira all at once. They were moments away from sending the Empire into disarray and hopefully giving their world the freedom she'd been so desperate for since she was a child.

The monitor built into the junction bulkhead whizzed through a series of code and subsequent menus.

"You're close," she said.

All the light throughout the corridor extinguished, along with the screen inside the maintenance junction.

Keller's eyes burst open, and he yanked the cable from his port. "Not close enough. They've rerouted all the power from this deck."

Alira gritted her teeth. "They know we're here!"

"And what we're trying to do."

A hail of bullets rained in from the other end of the dark corridor. One of Briggs' men fell, and everyone else scrambled.

Alira dragged Keller along with her to cover him from the incoming attack. "We have to get the hell out of here!"

THIRTY-EIGHT

"What have you done to me?"

Logan stared at the ceiling of the laboratory on the *Imperator* as everything spun around him. The sterile tones blurred into a mismatch of dull color, and the medical scanner's beeps became one synchronous whine. He tried to heave himself up, but he couldn't move from the restraints keeping him on the bed.

"Hello?"

Some footsteps approached, and he tried to take a look at the shadowy figure. If it wasn't for the pleasant perfume, he wouldn't have been able to tell who it was. But the powerful scent left him with little doubt.

"How are you, Captain Sutter?" Doctor Vanstrom asked, waving her medical probe over him.

"Why do I feel like this?"

"I assume you're referring to the dizziness." She placed the probe on the tray next to the bed. "It's a mild side effect of the medication we've injected you with. While it may not seem like it yet, your neural pathways are being readied so your current memories can be removed safely. I initially developed this as a less invasive alternative to prepare the pilots for the insertion of James

Sutter's memory engrams into their own minds. During the trials, I discovered by employing the method, there wasn't much damage. Due to its success, I theorized it might be possible to wipe a subject's mind numerous times. Something which was impossible before."

"Admiral Jones must've been very interested in that." The fogginess around Logan subsided slightly, and Vanstrom's face became clear. She was quite an attractive woman on the outside. Unfortunately, what was on the inside was as cold as an icicle. "That's how he figured he could get me back."

She rounded the bed, checking more of his readings on the wall monitor. "I'm not sure about the specifics. As you know, the admiral can be guarded. One would assume with your rehabilitation at home not going as smoothly, he probably lost hope. My new method, though, has given him and you another chance."

Logan winced at a headache coming on. "What will happen to me?"

"Hmm?"

"The procedure. How will it work?"

She stepped closer and hovered a tiny medical instrument above his eyes. "For now, I'll monitor how your medication has taken effect. Once I'm happy with where you're at, I'll begin the surgery. At first, the memories you've had as Nathan Logan, and those you've sporadically recovered from James Sutter, will disappear. I'll then implant Sutter's original memory engrams into your mind. Like the pilot you were introduced to earlier, you should wake up with all the recollections you had prior to the moment you left for your mission to the Outer Rim a few months ago. It'll seem as if you were woken from a long sleep."

The intercom chirped, and she pressed in the comms panel on the bulkhead. "Vanstrom here."

Logan couldn't quite hear who the doctor was talking to or what she was saying, but she gazed warily back at him.

"I, uh, very well, sir." Vanstrom deactivated the intercom and returned to his side, ushering over a pair of guards. "The admiral would like to see you on the bridge."

She removed the restraints around his wrists and ankles and let him up gently. He nearly fell over, but one of the soldiers caught him. With a few more steps, he found his footing and left the laboratory.

After a brief trip in the elevator, he arrived on the uppermost deck of the *Imperator* and was led through the large doors onto the bridge. A chill raised the hairs on the back of his neck. He wasn't sure whether it was from the cool temperature or if it was a reminder of what he'd witnessed in his previous life.

Near the viewport, Jones stood with his hands behind his back, gazing out at the fleet surrounding them. The guards nudged Logan toward him and held him by the admiral's side.

"How are you feeling?" the elder Arcadian asked.

"I could be better," Logan told him, still slightly queasy.

"It won't be long now." He nodded at the faint sparkle of light ahead. "Do you know what that is, James?"

Logan shook his head. "Should I?"

"I suppose not. I don't believe even Nathan Logan visited Tarook."

"The heart of the Outer Rim? The core worlds?"

"That's right. We're a step away from ending this conflict. With one fell swoop, we can send what remains of the ORC's forces into disarray." The admiral grinned. "Soon, you'll be able to enjoy this as much as I."

Fox paced from one end of the bridge to the other, doing his best not to appear apprehensive. Usually, he was quite adept at disguising his anxiety. Unfortunately, since joining the fleet at Tarook, it'd become an impossibility.

It felt like only yesterday that a few men and women sat around a card table and decided that it was time to take the fight to the Empire, spawning the birth of what became known as the Outer Rim Coalition. Now everything they'd built was about to be destroyed.

Hauser walked onto the bridge and went to his side. Through the viewport, a squad of corvettes passed the bow, taking up formation. It was one of many ORC battle groups that had recently arrived for what would be the Rim's last stand.

"Has there been any word from—"

"Still nothing on either front," Hauser said.

Fox sighed. For all he knew, Vernon was probably dead, and with him any slim hope their rebellion had to survive the incoming onslaught. "You know, when we started this, we thought we were so smart."

Hauser raised an eyebrow. "Sir?"

"To think we could take on the might of the Empire."

"We all understood it wouldn't be easy—"

"So many have died..."

"If you could ask the fallen whether their sacrifice was worthwhile, I bet they'd say it was."

"That's the point. We'll never know, will we?"

Hauser pointed through the viewport at the collection of ORC vessels still pouring into the system to join them.

"No one has to be here. But we are. All of us. None of us want to live groveling to the Empire. When they kill us here, those who survive will know we died fighting for a cause we believed in. When the time comes to rebuild, the survivors will know they can fight, too."

"I never knew you to be so poetic."

Hauser smiled. "I've learned from the master."

"Sir!"

They both turned to Lieutenant Styles at the scopes and hurried over to him.

The officer indicated the screen in front of her and the litany of bogeys appearing at the edge of their range. "They Arcadians are entering the system and are on an intercept course."

"My god..." Hauser muttered. "How many of them are there?"

"Enough to defeat us ten times over." Fox spun around to the viewport at the rest of the ORC fleet assembled for what would be the largest combat confrontation in human history. "One way or another, this is where it ends."

THIRTY-NINE

The moving abyss of the unknown greeted Vernon as he looked up from helm. While he hadn't detached from the Arcadian corvette, the shifting star field continued to move around him beyond the other vessel's hull.

A tickle festered at the bottom of his throat, and he coughed, trying to free himself from the sensation. Some blood spattered from his mouth and peppered the console. He quickly pulled a handkerchief from his pocket, wiping it as best he could.

The comms panel beeped, and he opened the channel.

"Alira to Vernon. Come in," she said from the Arcadian ship.

"Vernon here, go ahead."

"We've been boxed into a corner over here." The frequency crackled, and gunfire sounded around her. *"We weren't able to link to their communication array before they shut down the power to the deck. We'll need to get to the computer core. Can you tell us the best route to take?"*

"Checking now." Vernon fumbled at the controls and pointed the scopes into the interior of the corvette. He zoomed in on their location where two Arcadian teams closed in on their position and back out, locating the computer core. "You'll have to proceed down five decks."

"Five decks!"

Vernon examined the different routes. There was only one that might work, should Briggs and his men be able to get them there. "If you can get to the next junction and take a left, you should be able to escape through the maintenance shaft. That'll lead you to the computer core."

"We'll—"

Alira's broadcast ended abruptly, and Vernon tried to reopen the channel. He failed.

Jammed. Damnit!

He checked the scopes to find they'd taken his advice and were moving to the shaft. Vernon zoomed out and discovered yet another team of Arcadians on the march, but not in the direction of the Bolarans. Instead, they were heading toward his location. He could either unlatch from the Arcadian ship, leaving Alira and the others behind, or wait to be slaughtered in his cockpit. Neither option appealed to him.

There was one other course of action which was just as risky but might give all of them a better shot of surviving. Vernon opened his jacket and checked his sidearm, ensuring it was fully loaded. He got out of his seat and hurried to the airlock and through it onto the corvette. With the coast clear, he moved in the opposite direction to the incoming Arcadians and hid behind a corner.

The enemy soldiers soon arrived and pushed through the airlock. Once he was free to go, Vernon set off down the corridor inside the Arcadian vessel, stopping at every alcove, making sure he couldn't be discovered.

Around the next corner, loud footfalls clattered against deck, and a team of ten Arcadian soldiers rushed past him. Vernon stood deathly still behind his cover as they passed. None of them stopped, and the echo of their feet dispersed in the distance.

He breathed a sigh of relief and prepared to continue, but the swoosh of a door behind him opening made him freeze on the spot. His adrenaline kicked in, and he spun around, coming face to face with an Arcadian officer as startled as him. Vernon and the young man, with ensign rank pins on his collar, stared at each other for what felt like an eternity.

The ensign looked down at the gun Vernon had drawn and somehow found the courage to slap it from his hands. It tumbled to the deck, and the Arcadian grabbed Vernon by the shoulders, heaving him inside his quarters and tossing him to the floor.

The door shut, and the ensign attempted to find the downed gun. Vernon sucked in a quick breath and scrambled on his hands and knees toward him, yanking the younger man's legs out from under him and tripping him up before he could reach it.

The ensign grunted and cursed, flipping himself over and lunging at Vernon just as he'd regained his feet. The pair went flying to the deck, and they tumbled over the top of each other, wrestling from one position to another.

They crashed into a side table, and a vase smashed down from it. Vernon dodged the falling glass and pulled himself from the tussle, using what little strength he had in his legs to push the incoming man away and into the tiny dining table opposite them.

He glanced sideways at his gun and made a dash for it, rolling off his back and launching at him from his knees. But the ensign was quick and coiled a cord around Vernon's throat. He choked and coughed, spitting up more blood. He tried to muscle the Arcadian from his back, and the pair flung backward into the bulkhead.

Vernon grappled the other man sideways to break free. But his pesky opponent wouldn't let him go. Vernon's legs gave out, and he fell to the floor. With no air filtering into his lungs, spots appeared in his vision. On his knees, he looked around and caught a glimpse of a large piece of the broken vase.

Vernon put out his hand, but he couldn't quite reach it. He tried again, dragging himself and the Arcadian with him. He knew he was only seconds from blacking out.

Then he grasped the shard.

He swung it behind him, and the ensign shrieked. Vernon jabbed him again, and the cord around his neck loosened. He took in all the oxygen his lungs would take and turned to the Arcadian, yanking the glass from his kidneys. Blood spurted from the wound, and he gazed at Vernon with his mouth agape.

The uniform was a little different to back in his day, but he couldn't help but see a part of the man he used to be in the kid's features. The ensign's eyes closed, and he collapsed on the deck in a heap.

Logan didn't much want to be on the bridge when the Arcadian fleet and the ORC engaged each other, however, it would've been a damn sight better than been taken back to the lab. At first, he fought the guards who were tasked with taking him below decks, but he was in over his head. They dragged him all the way down there, and when he arrived, Doctor Vanstrom and her team were ready for him, decked out in surgical gowns.

He resisted again. Even if it was in vain, he had to at least try. The soldiers didn't let him overpower them, though, and grabbed hold of each of his limbs, carrying him to the table and strapping him down. The restraints dug into his skin with every thrust he took to break free.

"You can't do this to me, Vanstrom!" he yelled.

The hollowness in the doctor's eyes betrayed little emotion. She was no Freeman. What humanity might have been in Vanstrom was long gone. She was a product of the Empire, unlike the meek young man from the colonies of the Rim.

"That'll be all," she told the soldiers.

They filed out, and she examined Logan with her medical probe. "Very good. Your neural pathways are ready for the procedure."

Logan continued to fight.

"Please, Captain Sutter, save your strength." Vanstrom nodded to one of the nurses, and they approached with a sedative.

The soft hiss of the injection sounded, and his vision became blurry. If things went as Vanstrom and Jones had promised, soon he would forget everything.

Brindara. The war. Vernon.

Jana...

His eyes slowly closed, and he held on to her image. If it was the last thing he'd remember, the memory of Nathan Logan could at least die in peace.

FORTY

"The Arcadians are scrambling their fighters, sir."

Fox nodded, acknowledging Lieutenant Styles at the scopes. "Communications, send word to our own squadrons to move into a defensive formation."

"Aye, sir," came the reply from Ensign Van Berken.

Hauser approached from the combat station almost at a loss for words at the size of the mighty Arcadian fleet. "Are they just going to sit there?"

"They know they have us outmanned and outgunned," Fox said. "Every moment that passes only bolsters them. They believe the more anxious we'll get, the more likely it is we'll make a mistake and give them an opening to exploit. I'd do exactly the same if I were in their position."

"So, it's a matter of who blinks first."

"Perhaps we can beat them at their own game." Fox walked over to the scopes and peered over Styles' shoulder at the massive line of Arcadian vessels. "If we're to have any hope here, we'll have to knock out the firepower of their cruisers." He pointed at a particular grouping of the enemy contacts. "Their protection is relatively thin on that flank."

"Hit and run?" Hauser suggested.

Fox nodded. "Send in attack groups sixteen, seventeen, and eighteen."

She rushed off to relay the message, and Fox turned to the viewport. The attack groups maneuvered from the right flank and got underway toward the enemy line.

It didn't take long for the fireworks to start with the Arcadian cruisers returning fire on their ORC counterparts. Their line broke slightly, and Arcadian support ships entered the area, but not before three of their cruisers went up in flames.

"We're getting some action here!" Hauser yelled from the communications station.

The rest of the Empire's fleet shifted toward the first line of the ORC defense. Space lit up with the fire of the Arcadian arsenals as enemy corvette groups made strafing runs.

"Standby countermeasures!" Fox ordered. "Target the lead of that battle group!"

The bridge became a hotbed of sound, the voices of its officers echoing against the bulkheads. Through the viewport, explosions from the massive confrontation filled every sector above Tarook's orbit, while the scopes became a mess of ships exchanging fire, fighters engaging one another, and missiles whizzing between their targets.

The vessel shook from the ordnance pinging around them and their countermeasures snuffing out any major collisions with their hull.

Hauser went to Fox's side behind Styles. "They're boxing us in with their superior numbers. Their flanks are squeezing our outer side and making us bunch up. We need to spread our forces."

Fox pointed at the surrounding Arcadian vessels. "If we do, they'll pick our ships off one by one. These destroyer groups and fighter squadrons are just waiting for us to scramble."

She bit her bottom lip. "What do you suggest?"

He scanned the battle zone and tapped his finger against the screen. "Let's punch a hole through them here and force them to turn their attention away from our central forces. Instruct every ship in that area to make a run through their line. Tell attack groups five through twelve and nineteen through twenty-four to set a course to give them a hand."

Novikova trudged out of her quarters and took an elevator to the top deck. The doors swooshed open, and she entered a cacophony of noise filtering throughout the corridor. From one end were the sounds of the command officers speaking with each other on the bridge, and at the other, some techs and engineers furiously working away at the various maintenance junctions.

Novikova continued on and stopped at the door to the left of the entrance to the *Trailblazer's* bridge. She pushed on the panel beside it, and the door chime buzzed. A moment or two lingered, and it finally opened, revealing the ship's XO, Commander Telcourt.

She straightened her back as much as she could, considering the ache persisting through her bones. "I'm here to see Captain Waters, sir."

He glanced at the captain who was sitting at her desk, and she waved her in. Telcourt stepped aside and allowed her to enter, closing the door behind them. Novikova walked up to Waters and gave the CO a moment to finish stacking her data pads off to her side.

"Take a seat, recruit," she said. "How are you feeling?"

Novikova let a load off and sat on the chair opposite her. "I'm fine, Captain. I want to thank you for coming to my—"

Waters waved off the plaudits. "I just wish we could've saved more of your crewmates. We need all the help we can get at the moment."

Novikova peered past the captain at the stars whizzing by. "I understand we're returning to the Rim."

Waters nodded. "The Arcadians have pushed us all the way back to Tarook. Apparently, the battle has already begun. Hopefully, we'll be of some help when we arrive."

"That's what I've come to talk about."

"Oh?"

"I feel I'm fit for duty again. But since you're fully staffed here, I don't think I'll be of much value to you on the *Trailblazer*."

Waters craned her neck.

"I'd like to request a new assignment."

"A new assignment?" The captain chuckled grimly. "In the next few hours there may not be any assignments left to give."

"I believe Logan's aboard the *Imperator*, ma'am. I think we can both take a good guess that Admiral Jones's carrier will be at Tarook when we arrive. If it's possible—"

"Out of the question." Waters raised her hand. "Mounting a rescue mission at the moment is the least of our—"

"I'm not asking you for any help, Captain," Novikova interrupted her. "If you can lend me a jumpship, I'll mount the rescue myself."

"Recruit, you can't take on one of the most secured Arcadian vessels by yourself. I don't think you understand—"

"Captain," she cut her off again and spotted the wedding ring on Waters' finger. "I refuse to leave him over there with them. Please, just one jumpship."

Waters rested her arm on her desk and stared into her eyes. The pair shared a silent moment only two women could.

"Very well, you can have your jumpship. But if you get in trouble—"

"I understand." Novikova didn't hang around long enough for the captain to change her mind and quickly departed. In the corridor waiting for her was recruit Pitts.

"I wasn't aware you were back on your feet," she said.

"The doctor doesn't realize I snuck out," he told her.

"Maybe you should return to the sickbay." She reached for his arm. "Here, let me—"

He stopped before she could grab hold. "You're going to try to rescue him, aren't you?"

Novikova raised her eyebrows. "How did you know?"

"Because while I might be a bit of a bonehead, I'm not as stupid as I look. Did she approve your request?"

She nodded.

"Good. I'm coming with you."

Vernon peered around the corner, where two groups of Arcadian soldiers converged on a single focal point in the other direction. It didn't take long to figure out who their target was, with the Bolarans coming out from cover and firing back at them.

Beyond lay the entrance to the room containing the computer core. Now under heavy attack, the team he'd traveled with was getting increasingly hemmed in to the side with no way in.

Vernon wiped his mouth and reached for his sidearm.

Briggs and his soldiers were fighting valiantly, but they wouldn't last long. Vernon pulled the gun close to him and noticed blood smeared on his fingertips. He dabbed his mouth again, and more blood stained his hand.

It wouldn't stop bleeding.

Vernon closed his eyes and rested his head against the bulkhead. He'd known the end was coming for some time. He'd even thought he'd found peace with it, and that when his life was snuffed out, he'd accept it.

Not just yet...

He reopened his eyes and came out from hiding.

He fired.

One Arcadian fell.

He fired again.

Another soldier dropped.

The Arcadians caught on and turned in his direction. Through the hellfire, Keller and Alira stared back at him. With a knowing look, Alira directed the Bolarans onward, now having the diversion they needed. Briggs and his men covered them, and they ran for the computer core.

The Arcadians fired back, and Vernon dashed around the corner with a hail of bullets flying his way, only narrowly missing him.

The sound of heavy boots rushed in his direction, and Vernon reloaded his gun, ready to make one last stand.

FORTY-ONE

"We've lost attack group twelve and nine!"

"The left flank is breaking down!"

"Our fighter squadrons are getting slaughtered out there!"

Fox held station at the center of the bridge as the ship rocked from the explosions bursting around them. They'd taken a few hits of their own, but unlike a lot of their comrades' vessels, they were still in one piece.

"Send attack groups twenty through twenty-four to bolster our left," he said to Hauser, who was standing by the communications officer. "And direct corvettes *Velocity*, *Rising Dawn*, and *Corona Star* to take care of those fighters bombarding our cruisers."

Hauser gave her subordinate the instructions and hurried over to Fox. "Our lines are breaking down everywhere. It might be time to regroup."

Another explosion off the starboard bow rocked the hull.

"And where would you have us go?" he asked.

Hauser had no answer. She would've known as well as he did that everything had been leading to this day.

"Surrender is the only option left," he said, "and I

don't think any of our people would follow the directive even if I gave it."

Her face turned pale, and she followed him over to the scopes. "What if we move our destroyers back to cover our carriers, giving them a chance to launch more fighters?"

"Good idea." Fox glanced at the comms officer. "Do it."

"Aye, sir," came the reply.

Fox's eyes glazed over at Styles' monitor. "The mighty machine of the Empire knows no bounds."

Hauser pointed at the scopes. "They're making a push at our center."

It hadn't mattered what tactics Fox devised. The Arcadians kept surging back stronger and in more numbers. "If they break that line, they can make a run at the heart of our fleet. Once they do…"

He trailed off, not wanting to add to the gloom. Unfortunately, his prediction didn't take long to come to fruition. Several Arcadian battle groups soared through the center, destroying numerous ORC cruisers on their way.

Fox closed his eyes, and the quaking around them increased, with their countermeasures beginning to fail. He opened his eyes to the fury raining down on them, not that dissimilar to the holy tales read to him as a boy. In that moment, he wondered what part of the afterlife would be reserved for him.

Hopefully the Empire hasn't expanded that far yet…

"Sir!" Styles yelled over the carnage. "Look at this!"

Fox and Hauser gazed at the screens, and both their jaws dropped.

"Admiral!"

Jones unclasped his hands from behind his back and drew his attention away from the engagement above Tarook. While the deck shuddered from the occasional strike detonating in the vicinity of the *Imperator*, his vessel had remained mostly unscathed.

"What is it?" he asked his officer at the scopes.

"We've got several bogeys coming out of hyperwarp and approaching our position," the ensign said.

"ORC reinforcements?"

"No, sir."

It couldn't be any Arcadian battle groups, considering the bulk of his forces were tied up in the current confrontation. "Then who?"

"I'm detecting..."

Jones marched over to him. "Spit it out."

"Uh, I'm reading them as Bolaran and Thandeean, sir."

"What!" Jones examined the scopes at the scattered bogeys approaching. It soon turned into a much larger affair, with more popping out of hyperwarp with every second that passed. "How could...?"

Jones tossed the questions aside. It didn't matter right now. Obviously, the ORC had struck a pact with the Bolarans and Thandeeans. The repercussions of which would pose significant issues down the track. For the moment, he'd have to pivot in more ways than one.

He spun around to the viewport where his forces were mounting an assault against the ORC through the heart of their defenses. "Break off our attack on the rebel fleet and bring our ships about. Relay a message to our rear line to engage the incoming Bolaran and Thandeean vessels."

"Aye, sir," came the reply from the comms.

"I want to keep a squeeze on the rebels, so have the flanks give no quarter."

More acknowledgements followed as he reset the table for the next strike. For a moment, he felt like a young man again. While the Empire's conflict with the ORC had been a precarious affair, mounting full-scale invasions against the Bolaran and Thandeean home worlds were another matter altogether. Them joining the rebels would only make things that much more complicated.

"Sir!" His officer at the scopes swiveled in his chair. "The Bolarans have moved into an attack formation. They appear to be concentrating their forces near our carriers and fighter squadrons."

Jones did a double take at the monitor to confirm the use of the unusual tactic. "They know about our pilots..."

Alira erupted through the door into the computer core and stopped at the massive spherical mainframe at the center of the room. She held the increasingly unsteady Keller on his feet and hurried to the solitary workstation.

The Bolaran leader peeled the skin from his neck, and she attached the cable, plugging the other end into the Arcadian corvette's computer. Keller closed his eyes and rested his head back, flinching with every gunshot outside the door.

She shook her head, thinking about Vernon. He was a mere afterthought when they'd first met. Now, she didn't know what any of them would have done without him.

Keller groaned. "I..."

"What is it?" Alira asked.

"They've put up another firewall." He winced. "I don't think I have the strength to do this."

Alira would have liked nothing more than to yank the cable from his neck and throw it away for good. Unfortunately, he was their only hope. Bolar's only hope. The only chance anyone within the Empire's reach had at defeating their tyranny.

More bullets clattered against the outer door, and some of her soldiers scrambled backward. She couldn't tell how many of Briggs' men were left, however, there was no doubt the noose was tightening.

"They're getting closer," she said, trying to spur him on.

Keller pulled himself together and took a few deep breaths. Alira could only imagine what he was going through. Even when he tried to explain the experience to her, she never truly felt like she understood it.

More firepower cracked, nearly deafening her with its echo bouncing around the computer core. She resigned herself to the fact this was it. There was nothing more to give.

An explosion rocked the deck and rattled through her bones. She looked to the door, where a pair of her soldiers stared out with their mouths agape.

Briggs rushed in and waved her outside. "You've got to see this!"

Alira checked on Keller to make sure he was okay and followed Briggs into the corridor. She was greeted to a massive hole blown through the ceiling and beneath it piles of Arcadian bodies. "What the hell happened here?"

"Someone must've planted an explosive on the upper deck," he said, fanning his rifle around for any survivors.

Something clanked above their heads, and a leg appeared from the above, trying to get a footing on a broken beam. Whoever it was failed and came tumbling down in front of them. Briggs aimed his gun at the person, and Alira rushed to their side, flipping them over.

"Vernon!" she gasped at the man's gashed and gory form. "You did this?"

"I thought you could use some more help," he stammered from his bloody mouth.

"Your legs are broken!"

"And the rest of me."

Alira and Briggs picked him up and dragged him inside the computer core room. They lay him down on the deck next to Keller, and the medic checked him over.

"What's his problem?" Vernon asked.

"He can't break through the firewall," Alira said.

Vernon grabbed Keller's hand. "Hey!"

Alira glanced at the medic, examining the readings on his medical probe. He looked at her and shook his head, putting the probe back on his belt.

Keller's eyes slowly opened.

"This is it now, you hear!" Vernon pulled some dog tags from his pocket and grasped them tight. "There isn't a tomorrow for us. This is where it ends. Let's give the rest of them something to look forward to."

Keller gained a second wind, and a small grin appeared on his deathly cold face. The last shreds of his humanity shone through.

FORTY-TWO

"Jana?"

Logan opened his eyes, surrounded by darkness. Above, a slither of light poked through, and he shielded his eyes from its radiance. He ran his hand across the ground under him and picked up a pile of dirt.

Where...

Logan heaved himself up, and several green leaves whacked him in the face. He grabbed one and reached for the rest of them. They were cornstalks, at least a head taller than him. One step at a time, he pushed his way through them until he found himself out in the open. The heat from the sun was almost unbearable.

He'd never visited Gelbrana, but the vivid images Novikova had described were identical to what lay before him. He walked onward over a small rise until he spotted a house at the center of the farm. Climbing up on the porch, he took in the breadth of the property filled with corn crops in every direction.

Something squeaked behind him, and he turned to the front door opening. A woman emerged from inside. She moved into the sunlight and closed the door behind her.

"Jana?"

Her hair was tied up, and she held a manky old wide-brimmed sunhat in her hand. "Hello, Logan."

"What are we doing here?" he asked.

She smiled and motioned at the spectacular view surrounding them. "You're not really here. Neither am I. This is just a construct of your mind."

"I'm still on the *Imperator*, aren't I?"

"Doctor Vanstrom's conducting the surgery on you as we speak. This is what your brain has created as a refuge until the procedure wipes your memory engrams."

Logan stepped closer to her and stared deep into her eyes. She wasn't the real Novikova, rather the recollections of what he remembered of her. He took her hand, and the warm touch was there, just as he'd hoped. "I don't want to leave you."

A tear fell down her cheek, and she wrapped her arms around him. Logan refused to let go, clinging hold of her and nuzzling into her head.

In the distance, a fire ignited at the edge of the cornfield, and smoke billowed into the air.

"This is the beginning of the end, isn't it?" he asked.

She nodded. "Soon this will be all be gone."

Novikova entered the bridge and stayed out of the way near the rear stations. The command center of the *Trailblazer* was a hive of activity, with Captain Waters and Commander Telcourt moving between their senior officers, readying them for what was to come.

Over the speakers, the sounds of the battle at Tarook filtered throughout the bridge. The voices were frantic and the noise of the weaponry being exchanged fierce.

"Attack group fifteen, link up with twenty and twenty-one to engage the Arcadian right flank!"

"Carrier Behemoth, move into position and launch all reserve fighters!"

"Fighter squadron twelve has been lost! Request reinforcements!"

"Relay a message to the Bolaran corvette group for assistance!"

"The Thandeeans are taking a battering at the Arcadians' forward line. Send available destroyer groups to assist."

No one on the bridge of the *Trailblazer* batted an eyelid at the sounds of war. Much like the men and women of the *Defender*, they were all well-drilled. Some had been officers of the Empire before hostilities broke out, while the rest were given a crash course and thrown to the wolves. It was a testament to their character that she couldn't tell the difference between the two.

"Ma'am, we're approaching Tarook," the helmsman informed her superiors.

The broadcast ceased, and Waters and Telcourt met at the center of the bridge. "Bring us out of hyperwarp," the captain said.

The distortion of faster-than-light materialized into a normal star field, and the dark-green orb of Tarook appeared. An audible gasp went up, surprising even the command officers of the *Trailblazer*. There were more ships than Novikova could count on the backdrop of the Outer Rim's last stand.

"Activate all defensive systems and power up the weapon grid," Telcourt instructed the ship's weapons officer.

The bridge again transformed into a cacophony of chatter, with everyone focused on the job at hand. Waters turned, and Novikova's eyes met hers. "Go, recruit. Good luck."

Novikova nodded her thanks and dashed from the *Trailblazer's* command center. She rode an elevator down to the flight deck where Pitts was waiting for her. He opened the side hatch to their jumpship, and they both hopped in, making their way to the cockpit.

Novikova took the helm and powered up the craft. "Strap yourself in."

They buckled themselves up, and she retracted the landing struts, taking the vessel from the deck and launching it out into space.

The jumpship shook from the detonations breaking out around them. Random missiles whizzed by, and railgun fire clattered in a spray of chaotic perfection. Novikova took hold of the controls and steered away from the worst of it, checking her scopes and doing her best to search for their target.

"Are you sure we can find him in all that?" Pitts asked.

"We have to."

"The Thandeeans are pulling back, Admiral."

Jones headed toward the scopes and peered down at the group of vessels fleeing. "Very good."

"Should we send any pursuers?" his officer asked.

"No, let them run. We'll deal with them later and use those forces to concentrate on the Bolarans." He pointed at the screen. "Move these battle groups into the first line of attack. Once the Bolarans have tucked tail, we'll resume our all-out assault on the rebels."

Jones went back to the center of the bridge, with the vibration of the *Imperator's* deck rumbling beneath him.

As usual, the Bolarans were a thorn in his side. Luckily, they were a shadow of their former selves. Even at three against one, his forces were much too strong for the allied fleets.

"Uh, sir?"

He glanced at his communications officer. "Yes?"

"I think you should see this."

In no mood for riddles, he marched over to him. "What?"

The communications officer activated the screen in front of him, and an image appeared. It was of a man not that much older than him. He was badly wounded, with blood dripping from his lips. Behind him, a woman, who he couldn't make out, kept him from falling out of his chair.

"My name's Charles Vernon," he sputtered, bringing up some blood as he spoke. "I was once a pilot in the Arcadian Fighter Corps and went by the callsign Phoenix."

Jones recalled the man. He was a celebrated pilot. One of the best, if not the best, back in the day when the Empire had gone through its period of rapid expansion.

"I'm reaching out to everyone today because there's a truth that must be told." The old man coughed. "Some years ago, we were led to believe the emperor relocated from Arcadia and remained off-world to oversee the Empire. In the last few days, I've discovered that this assertion is false. In fact, the emperor died. Every citizen of the Arcadian Empire was sold a lie."

"Where's this being transmitted from, Ensign?" Jones asked.

"Unsure, sir," he said. "From what I can tell, it's being broadcast throughout the entire Empire."

"This was all devised by one man." Vernon winced and continued. "Councilor McCrae of the Emperor's

Council orchestrated everything. And why? So, he could take and maintain his grip on power using an elaborate hologram of the emperor as a front. If you don't believe me, you can see the proof for yourself. I'm transmitting all the information I have to every star system in the Empire."

The screen went blank, and Jones clasped the back of the chair. "What happened? Where did he go?"

"I don't know, sir. It might have been terminated at the source."

Jones paused for a moment, lost for words. He'd known Councilor McCrae from the day he'd graduated the academy and had been loyal to the man since that time.

Could what he said be true?

He didn't have time to wonder. He had to focus on what he'd come to Tarook for. And that was to end a war.

FORTY-THREE

"My god!"

Vernon's transmission winked out, and Fox leaned against the beam dividing the scopes and weapons workstations. "He did it…"

Hauser went to speak, but she was lost for words, as astonished as he was. Vernon might have failed to assassinate the emperor, but he'd delivered something even more worthwhile.

"Sir, a data packet's been transmitted from the same source as the message." The communications officer opened the file, revealing the proof Fox's old friend had promised. It had the location of the facility in the Magnus Star System, along with the specs of the advanced holographic technology. The evidence was damning.

He turned to the battle continuing to rage on in space around them. The Arcadians weren't letting up, continuing to push through the ORC lines. He could only imagine what the COs aboard those vessels were thinking, considering they, too, would have watched the same transmission, along with everyone else in the Empire.

"Sir, something's happening out there!" Styles informed him.

Fox and Hauser both went over to the scopes and examined the lieutenant's monitors.

"I don't believe it," Hauser said. "Am I seeing what I think I'm seeing?"

Fox did a double take himself. "The bulk of the Arcadian forces are retreating."

"But why, sir? Why are some remaining behind?" Styles asked.

"You have to understand, from the day of its founding, the Empire has been held together by the supreme power of the emperor's office. His councilors reported directly to him while overseeing the many provinces. Over time, they gained quite a lot of influence themselves. Councilor McCrae obviously wanted more. His colleagues would have seen the same broadcast as we did, and now they've told those loyal to them to stand down. Only those under McCrae's banner remain." Fox looked across at the communications officer. "Send out a message to the entire fleet. Tell them not to pursue the fleeing vessels and target the Arcadians loyal to Councilor McCrae who remain above Tarook."

The incoming fire around the ship steadied, and more of the Empire's finest scattered from the engagement. The Arcadians' forces thinned considerably, turning the tables in the ORC's favor.

Fox put his hand on the back of his weapon officer's chair and pointed at the closest enemy cruiser in their path. "Get me a lock on that ship and prepare to fire at will."

"Traitors!"

Admiral Jones did his best to keep a calm demeanor

while over three quarters of his fleet fled from the battle zone. Never in his career had he seen fellow officers stand down from a fight. "Open a channel to the *Centurion* now!"

His communications officer did as ordered, and a holographic image of the *Centurion's* CO, Admiral Collins, appeared at the heart of the *Imperator's* bridge.

Jones stepped toward the projection. "Would you care to explain yourself, Admiral? Why are you disengaging the enemy?"

"Orders have come through from Councilor Wynn," Collins said. *"Forces loyal to him are to return to Arcadian territory at once. Other councilors have handed down similar instructions."*

"You're turning your back on your fellow Arcadians. This is tantamount to treason, Collins."

"No, Jones. What's tantamount to treason is the councilor you're loyal to, using our fallen emperor as a pawn and installing himself into power. I'd advise you take a good hard look at your allegiance, because it might just be the end of you."

Collins' image disappeared, and Jones gritted his teeth. "Has there been any word from Councilor Mc-Crae?" he asked his communications officer.

His subordinate shook his head. "No, sir. We can't reach him on Arcadia or on any of the emergency frequencies."

Jones could only imagine what had happened to him. McCrae was shrewd, but even he would have been caught off guard at Vernon's revelation. If he truly had done what was claimed, the other members of the emperor's council would have done everything in their power to eliminate him before he could escape Arcadia.

He pondered his next move. His orders were clear.

But defeating what remained of the ORC fleet now appeared an impossibility. Tens of thousands of the men and women under his command were depending on the decision he was about to make.

"Sir, the ORC and Bolaran forces are converging on us," his man at the scopes said. "The Thandeeans are also returning to Tarook to join the fight."

It was obvious the enemy was boxing them in as he had when the two combatants had first met. The opposing vessels didn't take long to announce themselves and unleashed their arsenals on his ships. Everyone looked at Jones expectantly.

"Admiral, the rest of the fleet's hailing," the communications officer said. "They want to know their orders."

Jones clenched his fist and closed his eyes as a missile impacted the port hull and shook the bridge violently. "Open a channel to the ORC."

"Channel open, sir."

"This is Admiral Jones of the Arcadian fleet to all ORC forces." He opened his eyes and grasped the nearest handrail. "On behalf of the remaining Arcadians above Tarook, I...offer our unconditional surrender."

The command officers on the bridge remained silent, witnessing something that had never happened since the Empire's founding. Strangely, however, the rebels kept closing and continued firing in their vicinity.

"Any response?" Jones asked.

The communications officer checked his console and frantically ran his hands up and down his controls. "The message didn't send. Our communications array is down!"

More silence lingered on the bridge.

The only sound was of the missiles detonating ever nearer to their hull.

Then Jones laughed.

Everyone stared at him, his unbreakable façade coming crashing down.

He pulled out one of his Jontorian cigars and scrounged for his lighter in another pocket, lighting it up and taking a puff. "Who said the gods don't have a sense of humor?"

FORTY-FOUR

Novikova sprinted down the corridor of the *Imperator*, stumbling into the bulkheads with the hull of the great vessel being pummeled by its ORC attackers.

Pitts had his rifle at the ready, but none of the Arcadians passing them seemed to be in a fighting mood. Not one of them had given the pair a second look since she'd latched their jumpship onto the carrier, instead fleeing to their nearest escape pod.

"We can't stay here too long," he said, remaining a few strides behind her.

Novikova didn't particularly want to hang around forever either. At the rate the *Imperator* was being pounded, it was sure to perish sooner rather than later.

They rounded a corner, coming face to face with someone in a white coat.

"Hey!" Novikova yelled.

The Arcadian pivoted and ran in the opposite direction. Novikova chased after them and closed, leaping through the air and tripping them up on their face. She flipped her over to find a woman with her eyes bulging from the shock. Her name badge read 'Vanstrom'.

"Where's Logan!" Novikova demanded.

"I don't have to tell you anything!" the Arcadian snapped.

Pitts arrived next to her and pointed his gun in Vanstrom's chest. "Tell her what she wants to know!"

The doctor went pale. "Lower deck. Section twelve."

Novikova dragged her to her feet. "Lead the way."

"But—"

Pitts rammed his rifle into her back. "She said lead the way."

Vanstrom relented and took them via the nearest elevator to the bowels of the ship. At the end of a long corridor, she inputted her authorization, opening the door into a vast laboratory. Medical instruments were scattered over the floor and the advanced tech of Artemis Unit trashed from the attack.

Novikova ran to the bed at the center of the chamber where Logan lay unconscious. With the ship continuing to shake around them, she freed him from his restraints and gently touched his face. There was no response. "How do I bring him out of this?"

Vanstrom pointed at one of the medical trays still standing and picked up a syringe, taking it over to Novikova to examine. Not knowing what she was looking at, she had to trust the Arcadian woman. Vanstrom injected him, and a moment later, his eyelids slowly fluttered open.

"Logan, can you hear me?" Novikova asked. "Are you with us?"

He gazed around with a hollowness in his eyes. "Where? Who?"

Novikova's chest tightened, and an anguish deep inside her wanted to explode. She dropped her head on the bed, and her knees turned to jelly, giving way on her. A fountain of tears broke free, and she sobbed uncontrollably. All the moments they'd shared flashed before her. From the moment they'd first met on Brindara to the last time she'd seen him on the *Defender*.

His hand reached out for her, and she held it tight. A warmness permeated through her. "Logan?"

His lips were dry, and the word didn't come easy. "Jana?"

She raised her eyebrows. "Do you remember—?"

"I'm here, Jana." A smile appeared on his weary face but quickly disappeared when he spotted Vanstrom. He recoiled, and she raised her hands, staying well back with the point of Pitts' rifle in her back.

"You've got nothing to fear from me, Captain Sut... I mean Logan," she said. "I had to terminate the surgery early when the other Arcadians fled."

Novikova wrapped her arms around him, and they embraced. Neither prepared to let go of the other.

Logan walked onto the bridge of the *Imperator* with Novikova close behind. The command center of what was once an impenetrable war machine was littered with debris and broken beams.

He stepped delicately over the fallen bodies and stopped in the middle of the bridge where a face stared up at him from under some sheared alloy. The eyes were open, but they were filled with horror. Logan kneeled and heaved the debris aside, revealing the prone form of Admiral Jones. "To think, when I was James Sutter, I regarded this man as a giant. I thought he was invincible."

Novikova put a consoling hand on his back. "Luckily, he was flesh and blood just like us."

Logan yanked a cigar poking out of the admiral's

pocket. "I doubt the Empire has suffered a defeat like this before."

"It hasn't..."

They turned to another familiar figure emerging through the darkness onto the bridge.

"If it wasn't for the likes of you, none of this would have been possible," Fox said.

Logan stood and winced from the booming headache setting in. "Have you heard anything from Vernon?"

"No." What joviality there was in Fox's features disappeared. "We've been liaising with the Bolarans, but there's been no word."

Logan frowned, and Novikova held his arm tight.

"However, we have received news that the Empire's falling into disarray. The emperor's council has disbanded, and factions are forming between the various councilors. McCrae has been confirmed dead, and his loyalists are now being targeted. It's going to take some time for them to sort their mess out." Fox moved through the debris and stopped near Jones's body. "Eventually, though, they'll regroup, and we'll need to be ready for them."

"Then what happens?" Novikova asked.

"If the Arcadians haven't risen against their masters by then and we come under attack again, at least this time we'll have support on our side. Our friend, if he's out there somewhere, has shown we can work with those new allies."

Fox ushered them from the bridge, and Novikova followed him out. Logan stood at the threshold a few moments and stared at Admiral Jones, and everything he'd held so dear caved in around him.

Logan flung the cigar in the air. It spun end over end and landed next to the cold body of James Sutter's former mentor.

FORTY-FIVE

"Man, it's hot out here!"

Logan picked up a load of timber and balanced it on his shoulder, making his way to a flattened area of soil where the frame of the dwelling was being built.

"Wait until it gets to the middle of summer," Novikova said, coming up beside him with a saw in one hand and a drill in the other.

He smiled and wiped some sweat from his forehead with his free hand. When they reached the frame of their new house, he plonked the timber down and sat on the edge of the construction. Novikova joined him, dropping her tools and sidling up next to him. They peered out at the farm which had first been tended by her ancestors, generations earlier.

Unfortunately, there wasn't much of it left. The Arcadians had seen to that. What remained of the corn was burned to a crisp, and the house that was originally built a century in the past was now long gone.

Novikova handed him a canteen of water, and he gulped it down. Her gaze drifted to her parents' tombstones. "I wonder if they're looking down on us."

He offered her the canteen and put an arm around

her. "They are. And they're proud we're starting all over again."

She nuzzled her head into his shoulder, and Logan stared into the sky. The first twinkling stars of the evening were pushing their way through the ever-darkening sky. One of the sparkling lights was brighter than the others.

And it was getting bigger. And closer.

Logan stood and raised his hands to shield his eyes from the glare.

"What is that?" Novikova asked.

The object slowed, and its shape became apparent. "A jumpship."

The vessel continued to close and maneuvered over the top of the scorched field. It extended its landing struts and touched down on a part of the farm, which would've once been covered in corn crops. The side airlock opened, and a ramp hit the ground. A figure followed, stepping out and marching onto the Gelbrana soil.

"It can't be..." Logan muttered.

Novikova stood and put her arm around his waist. "Who is it?"

As she walked toward them, her features became clearer. "Hello, Logan."

"Alira?" Logan did a double take to ensure he wasn't imagining it. "I didn't think you survived Magnus."

"When the Empire spiraled into chaos, it gave us an opportunity to get out of there. We got lucky." She frowned. "At least some of us did."

"Vernon?"

"He, uh..." Alira cleared her throat. "Vernon died not long after we sent the message. He succumbed to injuries he'd sustained helping us fight off a small army of Arcadians."

Logan bowed his head, and Novikova gasped, holding him tighter. "What about the Makriak's Disease?"

"You knew about that?"

"He probably thought he'd hid it from me. He didn't keep secrets as well as he thought he did. I just wished he'd have told me before we parted ways."

"If it's any consolation, he was happy to go out on his terms." Alira delved into her pocket and pulled out some dog tags, handing them to him. "He asked me to give you these."

Logan stared down at them and clasped them close to his chest. "Thank you."

"It was the least I could do."

Logan looked past her at the door to the jumpship. "What about Keller? Did he—?"

"He died with Vernon." She squinted. "His human side rejected the technological components not long after the broadcast."

"I'm so sorry, Alira."

"Don't be. He's given Bolar a chance to govern itself again and gave the Empire the bloody nose it might never recover from. It was a small price to pay."

There was an emptiness in her eyes. The Bolaran woman was doing everything she could to bury her emotions.

"So, where to now?" Logan asked.

"Back to Bolar." Alira gestured to her jumpship. "There's much to be done. Much to rebuild."

"We know what you mean," Novikova added.

Logan reached out, and the pair shook hands. "Until we meet again?"

"No offense, but I never want see you again," Alira quipped. "If we do, it'll mean we'll have to once again fight the soldiers of the Empire."

Logan chuckled.

"I will say, though, if I had to, I can't think of anyone else I'd rather go into battle with." A hint of a smile appeared, and she turned around toward her craft.

Logan wrapped his arms around Novikova, and they watched the ship take off, disappearing into the sky. She pulled the dog tags from his hand and put them around his neck.

Novikova took them in her fingers. "Here we were, worrying about possibly hundreds if not thousands of James Sutters, when all it took to bring down the Empire was one Charles Vernon. I'll never forget him."

"No. Me neither." He smiled, and they looked back at the frame of their house. "Come on. This won't rebuild itself."

A MESSAGE FROM ROBERT

There's nothing more I enjoy than building relationships with my readers. You can join my Reader's Club for news on my latest releases, receive exclusive bonus content, get free ebooks, and be the first to know about special deals.

Join today by visiting www.robertcjames.com

Lightning Source UK Ltd.
Milton Keynes UK
UKHW010820250822
407828UK00002B/497

9 780645 138788